'Yaz is my favourite character with a great attitude.'
Aiden, 10

'It is very funny. You should really buy this book.'
Amber, 10

'The whole thing is based on adventure!!'
Amelia, 9

'I like how there are real people and events as well as things
that don't really exist like the snake god.'
Ephraim, 10

'I love the museum, it is very cool.'
Hunter, 7

'I love the Sphinx and King Tut.'
Lila, 11

'When is the next one coming out?'
Rosalyn, 11

'This book is brilliant.'
Stella, 13

'The visits to Ancient Egypt are totally exciting.'
Verity, 12

Bill Bevan

Time Thieves of Tutankhamun

Bill Bevan

Quantum Mystery Books

For Georgia and Kaya

ISBN 9-798-4291-2599-2

The cover and map have been designed and drawn with resources from Dreamstime.com, Flaticon.com and Visualdestination. Set in 12 point Palatino.

Quantum Mystery Books
Haarlem Mill
Wirksworth
Derbyshire UK

Map of Thebes

Apophis

Valley of the Kings

Tutankhamun's Tomb 1922

River Nile

Alleys

Luxor Temple

Tutankhamun's Palace

Avenue of the Sphinxes

Streets

Time Machine

1

Just Another Morning Like No Other

Johnny ran his fingers through his fringe of fair hair, then flicked it away from his eyes before his mum saw it and started the haircut conversation again. He'd managed to avoid the hairdressers all summer and didn't want to be told about it again right now, not when he was trying to hold on to the last few fragments of the dream he'd woken from thirty minutes earlier. He'd travelled back in time to Victorian London and had been walking along cobbled streets, dodging in and out of horse-drawn carriages, when his alarm had eventually got through to him. As he stuffed another spoonful of cereal in his mouth, he thought going back just fifteen minutes would be enough. That's all, just enough time to meet his best friend Ted, so they could walk together on their first day at the High

School. High School. The thought made his stomach turn. Maybe it would be better to go back to last September and put off High School for another year.

'I'm sure it will be fine, Johnny,' his mum called gently across the kitchen.

She had worried and fussed over him since he'd got up, at first raising his hopes that she'd let him have a day off, then dashing them with practical advice.

'You don't want to be late on your first day, and you still have to take Yasmin to the crossing.' She nodded towards Yaz, sitting opposite him.

'Oh mum, do I have to?' said Johnny, his dream of time travel finally evaporating.

Yaz was his next-door neighbour. She was dressed in her usual trainers, sports leggings and jujitsu club hoodie, and made a face to annoy him as she pulled her black hair into a ponytail one more time. Yaz was always adjusting her hair, usually sighing that it was so unfair her mum wouldn't let her cut it short. She had come round for breakfast and the walk to school together since her first year. Her parents started work early at their warehouse, which imported clothes from Bangladesh. They kept giving Johnny and his mum tops, shirts, trousers and skirts, which his mum put on a show of refusing but always accepted. Johnny was sure Yaz was old enough to walk to school by herself now. She was nearly eleven for goodness sake, surely she could crossroads and not embarrass him anymore. His mum refused to agree.

'But I'm meeting Ted on the corner. The High School's the other way,' he mumbled, his mouth crammed full of cereal and milk.

Yaz mouthed 'chubby bunnies' at him and he nearly choked, spraying milk and bits of half-chewed cereal across the table. Yaz recoiled in horror.

Ted had been on holiday for two weeks, and Johnny was desperate to see him again without Yaz in the way.

Johnny's mum sighed. 'Please don't speak with your mouth full. You can still walk her to the crossing, then head on from there. It's only a little bit longer. Now eat up or you'll be late.'

Johnny groaned, stuffed one last spoonful in his mouth, and scraped his chair back as he stood up.

Yaz leapt up at the same time. 'Come on big bro. Just another year and we can walk all the way together,' she said cheerfully and loudly.

Johnny cringed. Why did she have to call him big brother in front of his mum? 'No way,' he snapped, 'you can find your own friends to walk with.'

As soon as he said it, Yaz's face crumpled, which made him feel guilty. For a moment. Then he remembered all the sporty and martial arts friends

Yaz kept telling his mum about. Johnny thought sport was only good on the games console.

'Come on Yaz,' he said gently, grabbing his bag and jacket from the back of the chair. 'Last one to the corner is a rotten fish.'

'Bet I beat you, bro,' she replied, already at the door.

'Oh Johnny,' said his mum, 'do you have to wear that tatty old coat to school?'

Johnny froze. He thought he'd got away with it, but she'd spotted his dad's old puffer jacket. This was Johnny's prized possession, the jacket his dad had claimed brought him luck as a young man. He'd given it to Johnny when he left and had written a message in permanent marker on the label, 'LOOK AFTER ME AND I'LL LOOK AFTER YOU.'

'Erm, I just thought I'd wear it for luck on my first day.'

'Oh, go on then, but it really should be in a charity shop by now.'

'What's keeping you Johnny?' called Yaz from the garden.

'Sorry mum, no time to change now.' He dashed through the door, grateful for once that Yaz was with him, and chased her down the path towards the street. He knew he didn't have a chance of catching her as he dashed through the gate and turned sharply onto the pavement. Ted sat on the wall at the street corner, scrolling through his phone. Yaz was already halfway there, but at least Ted wouldn't care who won.

Yaz high-fived Ted as she reached him.

'You traitor Ted,' called Johnny. 'You're meant to be on my side.'

Then Jordan appeared.

'Hey, Armstrong! Beaten by a girl again?' Jordan snarled as he flicked Ted's head.

Yaz took up a jujitsu pose, but Jordan stepped past her. Johnny gulped. Jordan had made his life misery during the last year they'd been at the primary school, ever since Johnny had beaten him at a sports day race and then laughed. Johnny had one year of peace after Jordan moved to the High School and he'd hoped to avoid the larger boy for as long as possible.

'I've been waiting for you, Johnny.' Jordan bore down on him, blocking out the street ahead with his massive shoulders and large, square head. He had a flattened nose and ears that stuck out like bruised cabbages from playing rugby. Johnny realised it had probably been a mistake to shout 'see you potato head' as he'd run past.

Jordan pushed him and he fell backwards over the low wall that separated Mr Everard's rose garden from the street. Mr Everard was proud of his roses and didn't like children. Johnny reached out for something to grab a hold of but only managed to scratch his hands on the rose thorns as he fell. He banged his head and jarred his shoulder as he thumped to the ground. He was dazed and helpless, his shoulder hurt, and he could smell fresh, stinking, horse manure.

Johnny's legs stuck out over the wall and Jordan tried to grab his feet. He could see Ted and Yaz hesitate and then move towards him. Yaz looked like she was going to try a martial arts move on Jordan.

'Get off!' shouted Johnny as he kicked Jordan's hands away.

Then everything seemed to slow down. Jordan went into slo-mo and his words stretched into one long deep growl. Ted and Yaz stopped mid-stride, their faces frozen into masks of panic.

That was when things went really weird. First Johnny noticed that everything went deathly quiet. The birds stopped singing and the traffic was silent. Clouds, roofs and lampposts began to ripple and bend as if they were a giant curtain blowing in a breeze, while a loud, deep boom echoed across the sky like a tremendous heartbeat. The air just above Jordan's head somehow twisted itself into a spiral and screwed down towards him. He tried to wriggle away but was caught by the rose bushes. The spiral of air transformed into the outline of an arm that grew a hand as it reached past Jordan. Invisible fingers grabbed Johnny's left foot and pulled. He watched in horror as his foot disappeared into thin air. It had literally vanished. He screamed and tried to struggle free, but there was nothing to kick at, while his good hand only snared sharp, piercing rose thorns. His sore shoulder was rapidly becoming more agonising and that arm was useless. but he was pulled back over the wall and now his leg started to disappear too. He screamed again.

The click of a door opening behind him broke through the sound of the echoing heartbeat. Johnny twisted his head around and saw Mr Everard standing on the doorstep dressed only in pyjamas, a dressing gown and slippers. The old man stared, mouth open. He didn't look like he was about to leap into action and come to the rescue. Johnny knew he was on his own.

With a painful jolt, Johnny's back was lifted off the ground and, in a desperate bid to stop himself from totally vanishing, he tried to push against whatever this invisible thing was that had caught him. Both of his arms were numb with pins and needles and he could barely move them. It was hopeless anyway. How could he push against thin air? He closed his eyes so he didn't have to see his whole body disappear. Something inside him told him not to give up and he felt his fear snap into anger and his head fill up with the buzzing of furious bees. He tried to shake his hands back to life but the pins and needles became unbearable as the tingling began to pulse and vibrate.

'Get off me,' he shouted in frustration.

There was a flash of blinding light and an ear-splitting bang from somewhere nearby. Johnny fell back down among the roses, hitting the ground heavily. The invisible arm was gone, there was a whiff of a woody perfume and everyone moved again. Jordan almost fell over the wall, Ted and Yaz ran over to them, and the sound of cars and birds returned. What had Mr Everard done?

'What do you think you're doing, Jordan?' bellowed Mr Everard, striding across the lawn towards them.

Jordan looked confused as he looked up at Mr Everard, stared down at Johnny, shook his head and ran down the street.

'Are you OK? Did he get you? Where's your trainer?' Yaz and Ted fired a barrage of questions.

Johnny felt his head had been drained and was now slowly filling up with thoughts again, like a flat phone on charge. His arms still tingled, his hands were throbbing and bleeding, his dad's jacket was ripped and he could still feel the imprint of the hand on his left ankle.

Quick, shallow breathing told Johnny that Mr

Everard was behind him. Great. Now he had the street's top miserable old pensioner to deal with.

Mr Everard helped him onto the wall. 'Well, well, well. The day has come after all, Jonathon Armstrong.' Mr Everard was smiling at him. Mr Everard only smiled when he had bad news to tell. What was he going on about? 'You are like your dad.' Mr Everard looked as if he was about to say something else but stopped himself at the last moment.

'Did you see?' Johnny pointed at the empty air where the hand had been.

Mr Everard just kept smiling. 'Don't let Jordan worry you, he's a coward like all bullies.'

'Not Jordan.' Johnny waved at the sky. 'I mean all of that… whatever that was.'

Mr Everard held up a hand. 'You don't look too badly hurt. Better get along so you're not late for school.'

Surely Mr Everard had seen something? But he turned away and inspected his roses while muttering something about 'time to visit the museum' as if nothing weird had just happened.

Johnny tried to shake dirt and horse manure from his clothes, hair and face and limped after Ted and Yaz, who were already walking away. What had just happened? He had a sore head and could feel a bump where he'd hit the ground. Had he really seen and heard all of that or had he just been knocked out for a few moments?

'Are you OK?' asked Ted, looking grey.

'I'll live.' Johnny limped beside them.

'You smell of horse poo and you've left your trainer behind,' said Yaz, barely able to stop herself grinning.

Johnny glanced down and his brightly coloured left sock screamed 'something weird stole my trainer' back at him.

'I'll get it later. Let's get to the crossing before you're late for school and I'm in trouble for that too.' Johnny tried to remember what had just happened, but it already seemed as hazy a dream as Victorian London. 'Did you see the sky twist, did you hear the booming, see my foot just, like, disappearing?'

Ted and Yaz looked blankly at him.

'You knocked your head, Johnny.' Ted spoke to him slowly as if he was stupid. 'Maybe…'

'Maybe you saw things because you were scared,' said Yaz.

'Didn't you see anything?' Johnny shouted. 'Mr Everard. Everything in slo-mo. The invisible thing. Oh, forget it.' They obviously didn't have a clue what had just happened. But Mr Everard had seen it, and he had moved when Ted, Yaz and Jordan were frozen to the spot. Johnny thrust his hands into his jacket pockets and felt the cold pavement through his sock.

'At least it's not raining,' said Yaz with a huge grin.

If that was meant to make him feel better, it didn't.

2

Mrs Corabella and Mr Leadbitter

Johnny and Ted made it to school just as the bell stopped ringing to find everyone already inside. A teacher in a dark blue tracksuit and light blue sports shirt was holding one of the large double entrance doors open. He was lean, athletic-looking with a neatly trimmed short haircut and tiny moustache.

'Get a move on you two!'

Johnny and Ted sprinted towards the doors. The teacher let go of the door as they reached it, and Johnny had to put his arm up quickly to stop it from swinging into his face, hurting his wrist as it banged into him.

'New, are you?' barked the teacher.

'Yes, sorry, we're late.' Johnny was breathless from running.

'Yes sir when you speak to a teacher. Name?'

'Johnny, erm, sir.'

'Johnny Erm, are you? Full names!'

'Jonathon Armstrong, sir.'

'Edward Campbell, sir.'

'Look at the state of you Arm-strong.' Mr Leadbitter said his name slowly as if chewing it like a bone. 'You are covered in dirt, smell like a sewer and what have you done with your trainer? Detention. Both of you. Straight after school. Not a good way to begin.' The teacher leant towards him. 'Is it?'

This was obviously not a question thought Johnny, so he continued to rub his aching arm.

'I do not allow untidiness, slackness or rudeness. Do you understand?' Mr Leadbitter was almost spitting as he shouted each word.

They both nodded.

'That is, yes sir! Double detention.' Mr Leadbitter felt the collar of Johnny's jacket. 'What are you wearing Armstrong? That's your dad's old jacket, isn't it? You're not fit to wear this. Me and your dad used to be good friends. I do not want to catch you wearing clothes unsuitable for education again. Now get inside, turn left for the assembly hall and find out which house you're in.'

They ran down the corridor. 'I hope we don't have him for any classes,' said Johnny.

'He's scary,' replied Ted.

They edged into a large hall full of nervous first years sitting in rows and teachers lined up on a low stage at one end. A small, busy teacher with short black hair, bright red lipstick and a dark blue jacket with shoulder pads clattered up to them in high heels, clutching a clipboard.

'You're just in time.' She smiled and tilted her head to one side as she looked at her clipboard from her left eye. 'Names?'

She reminded Johnny of a bird eyeing up a worm. 'We're sorry, miss,' said Johnny hurriedly. 'I'm Jonathon Armstrong and this is Edward Campbell.' Johnny could see Ted was too nervous to speak.

'Uh-hum, uh-hum,' said the teacher as she ran the end of her pencil down the sheet of paper. 'Armstrong, Arms-trong, Arm-strong? I don't think we have you. Are you sure you're at the right school?' She looked at him kindly.

There couldn't have been a mistake could there? He remembered his mum worrying about whether he'd get into the local school with Ted, but she was always worrying. Had she remembered to apply for the High School?

'We do have a Jonathon Arkwright.' She looked over the top of the clipboard at him. 'Could that be you? What is your address?'

'15 Park Side Avenue, miss,' replied Johnny cautiously.

'Aha!' She exclaimed with so much enthusiasm

that she made Ted jump. 'As I suspected, just a little administrative error. You're over here to the left in Achievement House. You too, Edward. Your house is your tutor group. The other houses are Aspiration and Perseverance. I thought renaming the houses would lead to more satisfied students and better results than calling them after long-forgotten, town dignitaries. Who's ever heard of Curzon or Montague these days? I'm Mrs Corabella, your headteacher, and I've just started here too. We'll be learning all about the school together.' She gave a quick smile and turned to Ted. 'Your tutor is Mr Leadbitter, who is also your year's P.E. teacher and, I believe, very enthusiastic about it. He's just looking out for the last few waifs and strays arriving late so he'll be along in a moment. Now run along and join the rest of your tutor group. Oh, Jonathon?'

'Yes, miss?'

'Do put your other shoe on, won't you?' She quickly took out a small bottle of perfume from her bag and sprayed it in a large circle around Johnny as she screwed up her face. 'I hope for a change of clothes tomorrow too.'

Johnny's heart sank for the second time that morning as he exchanged grim looks with Ted. Their head of house and tutor was the teacher who had just put them in detention. Johnny didn't think he was going to like High School.

3

The Museum of Curiosity

As Johnny and Ted trudged slowly into assembly for the start of their second week, Johnny wondered what excuse Mr Leadbitter would find to put them in detention today and whether he'd strike during tutor time or P.E. Their house tutor stood at the side of the hall, scowling at everyone as they walked in. Mrs Corabella stood at the front, smiling 'like a bleeding Cheshire Cat' whispered Mr Leadbitter as Johnny passed by.

She stood in front of the year, wearing a smart grey dress, clutching her ever-present clipboard in front of her. 'Well, as you know, I'm as new to the school as all of you and I hope you are all settling into our happy little family. I'm sure Mr Leadbitter has told you of our visit to the Museum of Curiosity.' She lifted herself up on the soles of her feet as she said the name. 'I was so delighted to find out about the museum when I arrived here that I thought it would be just perfect for first year visits. You will be glad to know that we begin with Achievement House today.'

For some reason, when Mrs Corabella said the museum's name, Johnny vaguely started to remember something his dad had once said about work, but whatever it was floated away before he could hold on to it.

'Have you been to the museum?' he asked Ted.

Ted shook his head. 'Never heard of it.'

A slight frown creased Mrs Corabella's forehead as she looked at Johnny. 'I'm glad you agree… erm, please remind me of your name again.'

A few people giggled.

'Johnny Armstrong, miss.' He felt himself go red again. Why did she have to single him out as well?

'Oh yes, how could I forget?' She consulted her clipboard. 'I'm sure we'll find time to get to know each other a little better this morning. Now, Mr Leadbitter, please lead on.'

Mr Leadbitter didn't look at all pleased as he gruffly ordered everyone to follow him. 'I've taken the liberty of having a couple of the older lads help out, keep an eye on everyone.' He looked directly at Johnny and Ted as Jordan and two other boys from the rugby team sauntered up to them.

* * *

Mrs Corabella led them down a tree-lined road somewhere behind the High Street. Johnny realised he must have walked past the end of the road a million times without noticing it. He glimpsed one grand stone office after another, half-hidden behind high fences, tall hedges and imposing gates. Mrs Corabella stopped about halfway down the street, checked her clipboard, glanced around and pressed a bell set inside a carved stone gatepost. Johnny could just make out the words 'Museum of Curiosity' on a small, dull brass plaque. He noticed it had a screw missing. A tall wrought iron gate and railings topped with vicious spikes blocked the view of the museum. The railings twisted and coiled around each other to form the contorted shapes of snakes, wolves and dragons.

Johnny nudged Ted. 'Have you seen the weird fence?'

Ted shrugged then turned away. 'They're just old metal railings, Johnny.'

How come Ted couldn't see the creatures? Johnny tried to follow the body of a spectacular dragon that had spines along its back, a spiked tail and folded wings, but he couldn't see where it started or ended among the knots of crisscrossing legs, tails, fangs and wings. He heard the museum bell ring again, this time sounding more distant. The more he stared at the dragon, the more it looked like it was slowly slithering between the other creatures, and all of them were sliding around each other. He blinked and shook his head; he knew it was impossible, but the animals kept moving and he was sure he glimpsed the dragon flick its tongue out.

'Daydreaming again, Armstrong?' snarled Mr Leadbitter.

Johnny jumped at his name and looked around to see everyone already crossing a courtyard of worn paving stones towards a flight of steps that led to the most ancient wooden doors Johnny had ever seen. The museum was a sagging timber building, its peeling white-painted walls divided into squares by black wooden beams and dotted with low, rectangular windows flanked by wooden shutters. Each window was divided into three smaller windows, and these windows were crisscrossed with strips of lead to create a pattern of diamond-shaped panes. The thatched roof slumped and bulged like a giant sleeping dog. Johnny noticed a grimy stone, set into the wall above the doorway, carved with the names 'Blanke et Dee' over the date '1560 Anno Domini.'

'You better get a move on or you'll miss the wonderful museum,' Mr Leadbitter sneered as he pushed Johnny through the gate, Jordan snickering behind them.

Johnny caught up with Ted and the rest of his

class in a large entrance hall dimly lit with giant candelabras. There were large doors to either side and a wide wooden staircase that led up to a balcony with a balustrade that ran around the whole of the room. The walls were crammed full of glass cabinets packed with all sorts of dusty objects, stuffed birds and crumbling leather-bound books. Cobwebs hung in thick clusters in the corners of the room.

The class was gathered in front of the staircase, where Mrs Corabella stood next to an old man leaning on a shiny, black walking stick. He was dressed in a dark green tweed suit, checked shirt and a cravat. He wore a low top hat that had a clock in the front, its minute hand ticked slowly around in front of whirring cogs visible through gaps in the clock face. The man's eyes twinkled behind a pair of thick, round glasses and a smile split his grey beard as their headteacher introduced him.

'He looks about a hundred,' whispered Ted.

'Mr Horatio Merryweather is the Curator of the Museum of Curiosity and has kindly invited us here today. We hope there may be the opportunity to run a small, weekly Museum Club for those of you who are interested.' Mrs Corabella twitched her head around to look at the Curator.

Mr Merryweather cleared his throat and looked around the class. 'Thank you all for coming to our small, old, provincial museum. We no longer receive many visitors these days, so please do excuse the dust, but I hope you will find something of interest hidden in the nooks and crannies of our galleries. This is a private collection of objects found across the globe by antiquarians, archaeologists, explorers, scientists and scholars over the centuries.' The Curator chuckled. 'I always like to think that a visit to our modest little museum is a bit like travelling in time through all the periods of human history. So, if you follow me, I will lead you on a short tour of the galleries before we take tea.'

Mr Merryweather beckoned them through one of the doors. Mr Leadbitter and Jordan followed behind, muttering about 'the old nutter.'

Johnny and Ted walked, mouths open, through one gallery after another lined with dusty glass cabinets packed with treasures, each with a small hand-written label. They stared at Greek statues with missing arms, piles of Roman helmets, bronze shields from ancient Britain, the prow of a Viking longship carved like a dragon, Aztec clubs and feathered headdresses, and pirate treasure in wooden chests. Ted quickly scribbled notes about each display.

'It's like all the best bits of history in one place,' said Johnny. 'Did you see that gladiator's trident?'

'It beats the British Museum,' said Ted, looking around, puzzled. 'But how come it's all here and we've never heard about it?'

Johnny shrugged. 'My mum isn't interested in history. She says museums are boring.'

'Boring?' Ted shook his head. 'You've never been to a museum?'

'No, but I'd love Museum Club. One day a week off from Mr Leadbitter and all these places to find out about.' He was dreaming of time travel again. 'What do you think?'

'Definitely,' replied Ted.

They stopped beside another door, which led into a room full of old black and white photos and scrolls covered in hieroglyphs. 'Ted, how come this place is so big?'

Ted looked through the door and frowned. 'It must go behind the offices we saw. We don't know how wide the street is.'

'I reckon it's bigger on the inside,' said Johnny, wandering into the room.

'Impossible,' sniffed Ted. 'You've been watching too much sci-fi. My dad's always saying how the town's old buildings ramble around each other. I'm sure he would have brought me here though, we're always visiting museums. He took me to the Fitzwilliam Museum at Cambridge University, which he said was his favourite when he studied there. The questions you should be asking are how come there's so much here and why isn't this place famous?'

'Hey, it's Mr Merryweather.' Johnny picked up a pile of photos. The top one showed the Curator with a prim looking woman and two children, who looked like brother and sister. They were standing in front of a desert hillside with an old-fashioned car and camels in the background. In another picture, they were looking at Egyptian sculptures.

Ted turned one of the photos over. There was something scrawled in pencil on the back. 'It says 'Nov. 27th, 1922, Valley of the Kings.' It can't be the Curator then.' Ted paused. 'Hey, that's the date Tutankhamun's tomb was found,' he said excitedly. 'Maybe his father or grandfather helped excavate it.'

'Do you think his family have owned this museum for, like, ever?' asked Johnny.

'Maybe.' Ted was lost in thought as he looked at the photograph.

'Erm, Ted?' Johnny looked around. 'Where's everyone else?'

They went back out to the corridor. Their class was nowhere to be seen or heard.

Ted looked around nervously. 'Oh no, we're lost.'

'We can't be far behind them. Left or right?'

'I don't know, Johnny.' Ted glanced frantically in both directions. 'We're bound to get detention from Mr Leadbitter if we're late.'

'Come on, let's try this way.' Johnny jogged down the left-hand corridor.

They turned left at the next two corners then Johnny suddenly stopped. They had come to a dead-end in front of a door decorated with a large carving of an old clock.

'We're going to be in trouble now.' Ted grabbed his asthma inhaler.

'Don't worry, all we need to do is retrace our steps. It can't be that difficult, can it?' Johnny felt like exploring a little further. 'Let's just look in here first.' He pushed the door, but it didn't budge. 'Must be locked,' he grunted, straining with the effort to try and force the door open. He looked for a handle or lock, then a voice made him jump.

'Ah, Jonathon, here you are,' said Mr Merryweather. 'We have been worried about you. You do not want to miss afternoon tea, do you?'

As Mr Merryweather led them down the corridor, Johnny took one last glance at the door. He felt strangely drawn to whatever was behind it and was determined to remember where it was.

4

Tea, Treasure and the Magnificent Marmalade-Making Machine

Johnny and Ted followed Mr Merryweather into a long, high room crisscrossed with a nest of thick, gnarled wooden beams just below the thatched roof. Three windows pierced the orange walls and Johnny was sure they were the ones he'd seen from outside, but it felt like they were far too deep inside the museum. Their class were sitting in small groups around tables tucking into mounds of toast and drinking tea from delicate flower-patterned cups. Tall cake stands groaned under large piles of scones, cakes and sandwiches. Everyone was spreading the toast with thick layers of orange marmalade that seemed to glow. Mr Leadbitter, Jordan and the rugby players sat by themselves at one table, scowling at the other students and refusing to eat or drink anything.

'Welcome to the Buxton Room,' beamed Mr Merryweather with delight.

'It's like a Mad Hatter's tea party,' replied Ted, still frowning.

'Please do tuck in. I recommend you begin with the toast and marmalade.' Mr Merryweather waved them on towards a table as he walked over to Mrs Corabella.

Johnny and Ted joined a table with two empty chairs, where five of their classmates were greedily stuffing slices of marmalade-covered toast, scones and cakes in their faces. All of the plates, cups and saucers were old and totally different.

Ted picked up a butter knife. 'Well, I'm hungry.'

Johnny grinned, reached for the nearest slices of toast and soon they were both spreading them with bright orange marmalade.

'Isn't it delicious?' said the girl next to Ted.

'I've never liked marmalade before,' said her friend.

Johnny recognised them as Emily and Alisha from their class, though they had hardly spoken to each other. Ted blushed and muttered something which made the girls giggle.

'What's with the marmalade then?' Johnny managed to say between large mouthfuls.

'The old guy makes it himself,' said Emily.

'He's a bit potty, to be honest,' said Alisha.

'My nan's always giving us jars of her homemade stuff,' said Emily, 'and it's awful.'

'But this is delicious. Mad, ain't it?' smiled Alisha, crumbs dropping from her mouth.

'Completely bonkers,' replied Emily, wiping her face. 'Marmalade is for old people but this, it's…'

'My mum will never believe I'm eating marmalade,' said Johnny and they all laughed.

Ted's eyes lit up. 'What's that amazing machine over there?'

He pointed to the rear of the room where a massive contraption made of huge copper bowls, cylinders and pipes stood hissing and shaking. Clouds of steam occasionally erupted out of various vents. Four large copper funnels, full of oranges, spiralled out of one end, while four, equally impressive, brass taps at the other end were filling glass jars with hot, sticky orange marmalade. The machine was covered in all types of black-handled levers, dials and big green and red buttons. A huge clock with black Roman numerals hung from thick chains above the machine. The second hand ticked loudly.

Mr Merryweather interrupted. 'My dear Edward, I see you are intrigued by my magnificent marmalade-making machine.'

Johnny put his slice of toast down. 'Do you mean it makes what we're eating?'

'Just the marmalade, Jonathon. Four different vintage types from the past. One of my own inventions.' The Curator's eyes twinkled as he looked over his machine. 'May I show you something in our collection that is quite special?' Mr Merryweather beckoned them with a sweep of his arm towards a door in the wall behind the marmalade-making machine.

Johnny and Ted looked at each other, shrugged, and stood up.

Mrs Corabella rushed up to follow them, but the Curator put his hand up to stop her. 'Can I ask you to keep an eye on your students, Mrs Corabella? I thought so, thank you.'

Her smile faded as she gave a tiny flick of her head and turned away to bark an order at Emily and Alisha. Johnny saw Mr Leadbitter stare angrily at them as they walked towards the door.

They traipsed along one corridor after another until Mr Merryweather stopped in front of a large, strong, wooden door with thick iron bands running across it. He used the three biggest keys Johnny had even seen to unlock the door, which creaked and groaned as the Curator slowly pushed it open.

The dark room was gently lit by a dim, golden glow that shone upwards from a low, table-like, glass-topped cabinet beside the far wall. Johnny felt compelled to see what was inside, realising how calm and safe he felt as they walked towards it.

Mr Merryweather spoke quietly, his voice sounding as if it was floating above them. 'I see you have already found the subtle power of the Shield of Ages.'

The Curator's words jolted Johnny as if snapping him out of a daydream, and he stopped. Ted continued, smiling and transfixed by the golden glow.

'What is it?' asked Johnny.

'The greatest treasure in the world, perhaps all worlds,' replied Mr Merryweather. 'This is a gift beyond time that money cannot buy. Please continue, you should see it in all its glory.'

Johnny caught up with Ted, who was looking wide-eyed into the cabinet and gasped. A large round golden Shield was slowly turning on a bed of luxurious red velvet. The glow came from the Shield itself, rather than a light. It was the most beautiful thing he'd ever seen. Gem-encrusted gold bands radiated out from an ornately carved central crown, like the spokes of a wheel. Each gem was as big as an egg and they sparkled reds, greens, blues and purples as the Shield spun. The spokes divided the Shield into twelve equal triangles, six of which held six strange gold, silver, bronze and copper objects. The other six triangles were empty hollows with intricate patterns carved into them that looked as if they also had once held objects.

'Shiva's trident, an Aztec snake, the Great Zimbabwe Bird. These are all ancient symbols.' Ted spoke quietly and softly. He looked up at Mr Merryweather. 'But they're from different times and places.'

'Very perceptive Edward. They are the sacred emblems from some of the world's most ancient and mightiest civilisations.'

Ted looked puzzled. 'Why are they all on one Shield?'

'The Shield of Ages is far older than anything else you've seen here and the very reason the museum was established.' The Curator pointed at the carved pattern of a cross with a hooped top. 'For the Ancient Egyptians, the ankh was the symbol of life. It should sit here. This Shield is a quantum vortex and its purpose is to protect our world from attack by the Shadow Lord, a force of darkness that lives in another dimension. Sadly the missing pieces make it weak and the Shadows are closing in. How would you like to help me find those missing pieces?'

The question took Johnny by surprise. 'Erm, what?'

'This doesn't make any sense,' exclaimed Ted.

Mr Merryweather looked between him and Ted and seemed to have second thoughts.

'Anyway, we must be getting back, it is almost time to return to school. I've said too much but I wanted you to see our most prized possession.'

5

Back to Reality

By the time Johnny returned home, his mind still reeling from seeing the museum, the marmalade-making machine and the Shield, he found Yaz was already drinking hot chocolate in the kitchen. She was talking to his mum about her jujitsu sensei, who sounded like a sort of super strict teacher. The oven was on and his mum was standing by a kitchen worktop, typing at her laptop while also checking a pan of simmering water.

'How was your day Jonathon?' his mum asked anxiously. 'I was beginning to worry. Put your bag down and peel those potatoes while you tell me about it. Yaz was just saying about how well-respected in Japan her martial arts teacher is, her sensible or something. You should think about going along, you know.'

Johnny groaned. It wasn't fair. Why did Yaz never have to help with cooking? His mum must have read his mind as she told him, through a thin smile, that Yaz was their guest and they needed to look after her as her parents worked long hours. It was the same old thing she came out with again and again, and he knew better than to argue, so he furiously attacked a potato with a peeler, while Yaz smiled smugly and sipped her chocolate over a sports magazine. Johnny felt he spent enough time with Yaz as it was, without going to sports clubs with her after school. He dropped the peeled potato into the bowl of water then picked up another and hacked at it too. Anyway, he had something much more interesting to tell his mum than the usual boring school stuff.

'I've had the best day at school, mum,' he said as he butchered a third potato.

Yaz's eyebrows went up, so Johnny knew she was interested despite pretending to read.

'Oh I'm glad, Jonathon,' his mum replied while concentrating on her laptop screen. 'It's such a relief that you're settling in at last. What did you do that was so good?'

Johnny's words tumbled out as he rushed to tell her everything. 'We spent the day down at the old museum, I didn't even know it existed, how come we've never been, it's full of amazing treasures. We even had this tasty marmalade, I don't even like marmalade, and you're always trying to get me to eat it. It's made in a magnificent old machine by the old Curator, he's called Mr Merryweather.'

Johnny fell silent when he realised his mum had closed her laptop and was looking anxiously at him. What had he said to alarm her? She looked in the oven, arranged a tea towel on the oven door handle, and then slowly turned around.

'The museum?' she asked in a flat voice.

He nodded.

'Behind the High Street?'

Johnny looked at Yaz for some sign that she knew what his mum was on about, but she just looked back at her magazine.

Johnny nodded again and stared at the potato.

'What on earth is the school thinking of taking you there?' His mum shook her head. 'That Curator is an old fool. I thought he must be dead by now.'

'Mum, that's not fair.' Johnny spoke quietly, more to the potatoes than to his mum. 'Mr Merryweather is nice. School's starting a Museum Club and I've signed up.'

His mum sighed and turned her attention back to the oven. 'You just be careful. He's dangerous, that's what he is. The water's ready for those potatoes so get them in the pan, what's left of them.'

'The museum sounds great Johnny, can I come too?' whispered Yaz.

He glared at her. 'No.'

6

Who's That Knocking in the Egyptian Room?

Johnny looked around his eleven school friends as they followed Mrs Corabella down the street towards the museum. Six girls and six boys had signed up for Museum Club. Mr Merryweather waited for them by the open door, dressed in a black tailcoat, bow tie and top hat that reminded Johnny of the gentlemen who had appeared in his dream of Victorian London. Mrs Corabella led them up the steps, where the Curator shook her hand and spoke to her as they all filed past. Johnny and Ted were the last in and they could hear the Curator and their headteacher arguing quietly.

'What's that all about then?' whispered Ted.

As they stood in the entrance hall gaping at the columns and exhibits around them, Johnny felt a sense of coming home, as if he somehow belonged here and could relax.

'Welcome you all to our very first Museum Club,' said Mr Merryweather.

'Where's Mrs Corabella?' asked Alisha.

'She won't be joining us,' replied the Curator. 'I explained to your headteacher that she won't be needed during the Club, especially when she has so much important work to do back at your school.'

Alisha and Emily glanced nervously at each other, and Ted looked worried, but Johnny was delighted. No teachers!

'Let us begin with a nice cup of tea, please follow me.' With that, Mr Merryweather swept out of the entrance hall.

Ted raised his eyebrows as if to say the Curator was a bit mad, as they followed behind. Mr Merryweather pushed aside a tapestry and they found themselves once again in the room with the marmalade-making machine. 'Please do come along, we have plenty to discuss and do today.'

The tables were again laden with teapots, cake stands, toast racks and marmalade pots. Twelve flowery plates, cups and saucers were set out waiting for them. This time, swords, helmets, shields and other weapons were scattered all over the tables or propped up against the walls.

'I do apologise for the state of the Buxton Room.' Mr Merryweather marched up to the nearest table.

'We have recently acquired a collection of medieval weapons and have such little space to organise things while we catalogue them, that I thought you might like to see the objects.'

Everyone rushed forward and grabbed swords or tried on helmets. Ted stood with a shield in his hands and looked at it open-mouthed, 'These are better than anything I've seen at the British Museum or Warwick Castle. It's just, well, it all looks so new.'

Johnny struggled with the weight of a dented and scratched sword. 'Wow, these are cool.'

'And dangerous,' said Mr Merryweather, who took the sword from his hands. 'I suggest taking extra care with King Richard's sword, Jonathon. It is still as sharp as the day it was wielded on the Bosworth battlefield centuries ago. Sad to say, Richard died soon after he used this particular sword to kill the Duke of Suffolk's son.'

Ted's mouth gaped open even further. 'You, you mean Richard the Third?'

'Indeed I do, Edward. It was rumoured to have been stolen from his body by Henry Tudor himself.'

Johnny laid it gently down on the table. 'It must be worth thousands of pounds.'

'Millions actually, but I was able to acquire it from a family in Wales who had no idea of its true worth.' The Curator shook his head. 'If only they'd known they were descended from Henry the

Seventh. Now, everyone please sit down and I will explain what you will be doing in Museum Club. The tea should still be nice and hot, and please do help yourself to plenty of toast and marmalade, then you can all treat yourselves to a slice of cake.'

As they munched toast and sipped cups of astonishingly strong, dark-brown tea, Mr Merryweather explained how they would be expected to dust, write catalogue cards and measure the objects. They had thousands of artefacts acquired by curators over the years and they needed recording before either being put on display or returned to their rightful owners. Johnny didn't think this sounded quite as exciting as handling swords and other treasure, though he reminded himself that it meant one day a week away from school. Ted nodded eagerly at everything the Curator told them and was the only one to make notes. Suddenly, Johnny realised Mr Merryweather was saying his name.

'Drink up Jonathon, let's visit the mummies.'

* * *

The room was full of rows and rows of brightly painted Egyptian coffins, each the shape of a person, with a blue and gold striped headdress and a colourful portrait of a face. They had their arms crossed over their chests and held sticks, one ending in a hook, the other a tassel. The coffins were painted with eyes, birds and hooped crosses.

Ted told everyone how Ancient Egypt was an African civilisation, one of the greatest there had been and that it had influenced Europeans like the Greeks and Romans who pinched all of Egypt's best ideas. He reeled off a list of Pharaohs and important places such as the Sphinx, Great Pyramids, Luxor, Karnak and the Valley of the Kings.

'These sarcophagi, or coffins as you may call them, contain the mummified bodies of Egyptian pharaohs, princesses, priests and ministers.' Mr Merryweather led them on a tour through the coffins.

'Urgh,' said Emily, 'like, there's dead bodies in them?'

'Well yes,' said the Curator, looking bemused by Emily's question as he tapped the head of the nearest coffin. 'There would be little point having them otherwise. This chap was Ay, he was Grand Vizier to Tutankhamun and then became Pharaoh in his own right after Tutankhamun died.' Mr Merryweather leant towards them and lowered his voice as if sharing a secret. 'Some believe he murdered Tutankhamun to take the crown.'

'I read that,' exclaimed Ted. 'But I've got a question.'

'Yes, Edward?'

'They look so new as if they'd been made just yesterday.'

''Another good observation Edward,' said Mr Merryweather.' The dry Egyptian desert keeps things in tip-top condition. We are conducting a few scientific experiments on these before we return them to their real owners in Egypt. Now, back to who killed Tutankhamun. I am afraid that we will never be sure.'

Mr Merryweather continued through the room, pointing at different sarcophagi as he passed by. 'All of the bodies have been preserved with chemicals, except for their organs, such as the brain, heart, lungs, which were taken out when they were mummified. The Ancient Egyptians had an ingenious way of removing the brain through the dead person's nose with a spoon. Just like you would use for an ice cream sundae. They used the spoon to break down the brain and scrape out the inside of the skull. Oh dear, are you all right Emily?'

Emily was looking decidedly pale and cupped her hand over her mouth.

'Perhaps a bucket would be in order?' Mr Merryweather handed a grey metal bucket to Emily, who turned away to be loudly sick.

Just then the lights went out, plunging the room into darkness. Johnny jumped, Ted made a nervous whimper, and everyone else screamed.

'Oh dear, so sorry,' said Mr Merryweather, lighting a candle that he fished out from his pocket. It lit their faces with an orange glow but left the rest of the room in the flickering darkness of moving shadows. 'This is the problem with such an old building. Someone has probably put the kettle on.'

The Curator was interrupted by a knocking that came from the far end of the room. He spun around in the direction of the sound, leaving them in darkness. Johnny felt the hairs on the back of his neck stand on end, while everyone screamed again, and they all huddled closer together.

'What was that?' asked Johnny, not sure he wanted to know.

They all jumped as the tapping came again, three clear knocks like someone banging on a door. A movement in the shadows caught Johnny's eye. He thought he saw someone moving at the other end of the gallery. Again, three taps rang out across the room and Johnny definitely saw one of the upright sarcophagi rock backwards and forwards in the gloom. He felt the urge to go and find out what was causing the sound but knew from horror films that was never a good idea.

Mr Merryweather cleared his throat and walked down the gallery to where the sound had come from.

'Don't leave us in the dark,' shouted Alisha.

The Curator kept walking, lighting up one sarcophagus after another with his candle as he stared at each in turn.

'Can mummies really come alive like in films?' asked Johnny.

'I was sure they couldn't,' sniffed Ted.

After what seemed like hours, Mr Merryweather paused next to the coffin of the man who had supposedly murdered the Pharaoh. Maybe he hadn't liked it when the Curator knocked on his head, thought Johnny. Mr Merryweather held his hand up in front of the painted face while muttering under his breath, then shook his head, as if to clear it. The lights flickered back on and bathed the room in welcome electric light.

'As I thought,' smiled Mr Merryweather when he'd walked back to them. 'Just air in the water pipes. Time to return to school, I think.'

7

The Time Machine

As Johnny and Ted began their third week at Museum Club, the dragons, wolves and snakes reassuringly wound and slithered in the railings as they walked through the gate. Johnny pointed out his favourite dragon to Ted, but Ted still couldn't see them.

They were soon sorting through treasure from a pirate's chest and Johnny decided to ask Mr Merryweather about the railings. 'Do you know your railings move?'

'I beg your pardon, Jonathon, they do what exactly?' Mr Merryweather sounded incredulous.

'He keeps going on about them,' said Ted, who rolled his eyes.

Johnny wished he hadn't said anything now. 'Nothing.'

'You can see the creatures of the railings move?' asked Mr Merryweather.

Ted now snorted with laughter and Johnny nodded in embarrassment.

'There are only a few people who see their true form.' Mr Merryweather furrowed his brow. 'What with the reaction of the Shield to both of you and now this, I do believe it is time to show you another invention. It might also answer your question about the mummies, Edward. Come along.'

'He's so annoying,' Ted said under his breath as they left the room.

Johnny and Ted half-ran to keep up with Mr Merryweather as he strode down a corridor, and they almost lost him as he abruptly turned left down yet another corridor. He stopped in front of the door with the clock face carved in it that they'd found during their very first visit to the museum. The hands were carved to show the time at quarter past six yet Mr Merryweather slowly turned the long hand to point at 11 and the shorthand to just before 5.

'Five to five,' mouthed Johnny. He couldn't see how the Curator was able to move the hands.

The Curator flicked a switch and a heavy-looking chandelier in the centre of the ceiling slowly lit up to reveal an old-fashioned room decorated with dark red-and-gold patterned wallpaper and matching red velvet curtains across a window. There was a second door to their left. A gramophone, a giant hourglass and a strange brass instrument that looked a bit like a short telescope attached to a curved ruler stood on a large wooden table. There were more weird, old-fashioned scientific instruments on other tables dotted around the room, which echoed to the heavy, slow tick-tock of a grandfather clock in the corner. Johnny briefly wondered why it had three pairs of hands. The far end of the room had bunk beds, a wardrobe and another door, with a small, painted sign that read Bathroom.

A giant globe, taller than him and Ted, and surrounded by four leather, wingback chairs stood on an ornately patterned rug in the middle of the room. Its continents and seas were brightly painted and had detailed pictures of pyramids, old temples, jungles, deserts, mythical beasts, sailing ships and sea monsters. This fabulous world slowly rotated in a polished wooden cradle with a wide rim around the Equator. The rim was finished with a low, brass railing and had various buttons, levers and dials set into it. A row of eight black rectangles was set into a brass frame. The first two were blank, while the other three spelt N-O-W. Everything was covered in a thick layer of dust. It looked like no one had been in here for a very long time.

'Wow,' said Johnny, 'it's like that old film about the Victorian Time Machine.'

Mr Merryweather chuckled.

'It's just an old study, Johnny,' replied Ted.

'Edward,' said Mr Merryweather sternly, 'it may look like an old room but it is a room beyond time. Jonathon, you are referring to the story by Mr H.G. Wells, I believe.'

'Yeah. Some bloke in an old suit travelled into the future and met a load of creepy creatures called Morlocks.'

'Well, what if I were to tell you this room was his actual Time Machine, one of the many experiments he based his novels on, and that it offers you the chance to visit any of the places and ages found in this museum?'

Ted raised an eyebrow. 'I'd have to say you're making that up Mr Merryweather, no offence meant, sir.'

'No, no,' said the Curator as he walked to the globe and hourglass, 'and none taken. I can imagine it is a difficult idea to believe in. Perhaps it is best to demonstrate. Remember Tutankhamun?'

They both nodded.

'Then let us meet the archaeologist who found him!'

Ted looked shocked. 'Howard Carter? But he's been dead for years.'

'Indeed, Edward. The Time Machine will enable us to visit the famous Egyptologist on a special day for him.'

Mr Merryweather took out a small silver egg. 'This little device will tell us whether the marmalade can protect you from the time shift.' He held the egg up to each of them in turn and it beeped and blinked a green light contently. 'As I thought, you are time travellers. Shall we go to the Valley of the Kings?'

'Oh go on,' scoffed Ted disbelievingly, then he turned to Johnny and whispered, 'he's obviously obsessed that his father or grandfather worked with Howard Carter. Let's humour him then get back to the others when nothing happens.'

The Curator pressed buttons and pulled levers on top of the wooden rim around the globe's equator, and turned the hourglass over. The continents, oceans and pictures all faded away to reveal a swirling pattern of red and yellow glowing clouds that welled up from deep within the centre of the globe. A low hum and a worrying rattle grew louder as the red and yellow clouds gathered speed and mixed until they became a blur of orange light that bathed the whole room in an eerie glow. The eight black rectangles were rapidly flipping over with a clicking sound, replacing the letters N-O-W with numbers that were counting backwards. The fifth rectangle quickly stopped on 1, followed by the sixth on 9, and the seventh and eighth both on 2. Johnny covered his ears as the humming and rattling became almost too loud to bear. They were showered in dust and a spider fell, on a thread, from one of the cobwebs in the ceiling. It felt like the whole room was going to shake apart at any moment. Ted was kneeling on the floor with his fingers in his ears, looking up at Johnny in fear.

Johnny jumped as Mr Merryweather shouted over the din. 'Sorry, the old thing hasn't been out for a spin in a long time. Just blowing some cobwebs loose!

The shaking and humming quietened to silence, the globe's clouds became dull and still, and the map returned with a large cross over the middle of Egypt. The clicking white numerals of the counter slowed down to stop on 2–7-1-1-1-9-2-2.

Mr Merryweather took them over to the wardrobe and started digging around amongst all sorts of clothes. 'Here we are. I'm afraid these Old Barovian Grammar School blazers aren't designed for the heat, but you'll look the part for 1922. Just put them on over your tops.'

Ted glanced at Johnny. 'This isn't really happening, you know that don't you, Johnny?'

Mr Merryweather put his hand on the door handle and smiled. 'Let's not be late for the big event.'

8

At the Tomb of Tutankhamun

Mr Merryweather opened the Time Machine's other door. 'Jonathon, Edward, welcome to Egypt, 27th November 1922. History is about to be made; or, more accurately, discovered.'

Johnny followed the Curator into the warm shade of a large canvas tent filled with shovels and spades.

'This is a set-up,' whispered Ted. 'It's just a big old tent with some TV lights outside to make it look sunny and some builder's sand sprinkled on the floor. I bet there's nothing outside.'

'Why would Mr Merryweather do this?' asked Johnny. He couldn't see why the Curator would go to so much trouble.

'It's a scam, got to be,' replied Ted. 'He's after money from gullible parents fooled into thinking they and their kids can go time travelling.'

'But the objects in the museum must be worth

millions.'

'I'm beginning to think they're all fakes.'

'That doesn't make any sense,' replied Johnny.

'And time travel does?' sneered Ted.

Johnny and Ted jumped as a stern, Welsh, voice spoke to them from the far side of the tent. 'Oh Professor Merryweather, this heat is all too much.'

They hadn't noticed the woman, who was sitting in a canvas chair. She had a wide-brimmed hat and a white blouse done up at her neck with a brooch. A boy and girl sat in chairs next to her. Johnny nudged Ted. They were the children from the photograph.

Mr Merryweather lifted his hat. 'Good afternoon Miss Price, it is a trifle warm.'

'I'm bored, nanny.' The girl slumped in her chair with her arms folded.

'Why can't we be with daddy in Cairo?' whinged the boy.

'Hush now,' sighed Miss Price. 'Professor, is there any news of when the tomb will be opened? The children are eager to visit.'

Mr Merryweather shuffled and fidgeted. 'Well, yes, of course, well, I am on my way now to, well, enquire on progress. Their uncle is at the tomb, I presume?'

'Lord Caernarvon has been there quite a while,' replied Miss Price curtly.

'You promised us a tour,' said the girl.

'Do wait here until my return, the sun is extremely harsh on young skin.' The Curator ushered Johnny and Ted hurriedly in front of him. He seemed eager to leave Miss Price.

As soon as they stepped outside, Johnny was hit by the blinding sun and scorching heat. He and Ted stumbled behind the Curator across broken rocks and sand towards a dirt road leading into a narrow ravine. An old sand-covered car slowly chugged along the road behind a line of camels, kicking up a choking cloud of dust.

'This is impossible,' gasped Ted, loosening his tie to breathe.

'Feels real to me Ted, I'm boiling.' Johnny felt the heat suck the breath from his lungs.

Mr Merryweather stopped by a man with an old-fashioned camera on a tripod. 'Do catch up,' he called to them. 'Let's make time for a photograph.'

'You know what this means?' said Johnny.

Ted looked at him blankly.

Johnny smiled. 'We're going to replace those two in the photo.'

'We can't,' said Ted. 'We've seen the photo. It already exists. The past can't be changed.'

'It was in *Back to the Future*,' replied Johnny. He knew that would annoy Ted.

The photographer planted the legs of the tripod in the sand and stuck his head into a large, black hood on the back of the camera. Mr Merryweather stood in the middle, a hand on each of their shoulders. Just like the original photo, realised Johnny.

'Say Tutankhamun's gold.' The photographer's voice was muffled by the hood.

They all looked at the camera, which clicked when they all mouthed the word 'gold'.

'Excellent,' said the photographer as he reappeared, blinking in the sunlight. 'I'll have it processed in my mobile darkroom later today. We'd better go to the excavation before we're too late.' He gathered up his tripod, lifted it over his shoulder and trotted into the ravine.

They followed him as quickly as the heat allowed and soon reached a knot of people crowded around a rectangular hole in the rock. Johnny saw a very large, grey-haired aristocratic European with a ridiculous handlebar moustache and a pith helmet standing arm-in-arm with a younger woman holding a parasol. He was deep in conversation with a distinguished-looking Egyptian and another European man dressed in a sand-covered white jacket and black trousers, who was brandishing a chisel. The photographer was on the edge of the group, once again buried under the camera's hood.

Mr Merryweather marched them straight up to the man with the chisel. 'My dear Carter, are we still in time?'

The man pointed the chisel at the Curator and laughed. 'You are always in time Mr Merryweather, are you not?'

Mr Merryweather gave a short bow. 'Lord Caernarvon, Lady Evelyn, Mr Ahmed. A pleasure to meet you all once again.'

Ted muttered, 'OK, this is getting weird. This is the day Howard Carter officially opens Tutankhamun's tomb for his funder and the Head of Egyptian Antiquities.'

'Gentlemen, lady, I invite you to follow me for the moment of truth.' Howard Carter turned and walked down a short flight of stone steps that led into the hole.

Everyone quickly followed behind, pushing Johnny and Ted to the back. Johnny glimpsed stone doors at the bottom of the steps.

Howard Carter stood with his back to the door. 'If my research is correct, we will have the honour of being the first people to see inside Tutankhamun's tomb since the boy Pharaoh was buried in 1323 BC. Here we can see that the doors are still sealed shut. I will chisel away the mortar and prise them open.'

He gouged the chisel into the tight gap between the two doors until a pile of mortar lay at his feet. He pushed the doors and they had opened just a crack when a rush of warm wind surged out of the tomb, accompanied by a roaring sound similar to a jet engine. It blew the gentlemen's hats and Lady Evelyn's parasol away. Howard Carter staggered backwards into Lord Caernarvon.

Johnny heard the faint sound of a heartbeat and was sure he could smell the same hint of perfume he'd sensed when he lost his trainer.

The Egyptian archaeologist exclaimed it was the curse of the mummy and started praying, Lord Caernarvon said 'My God' and Lady Evelyn swooned into her father's arms.

'The Curse of Tutankhamun, Ted!' Johnny remembered the story. 'Everyone at the dig site dies within a few years.'

'There's a simple scientific explanation,' said Ted and Howard Carter together.

Howard Carter smiled and nodded briefly to Ted. 'There is no need to panic everyone. It is just a difference in air pressure between the tomb and outside. Completely normal. Have you recovered, Lady Evelyn?'

Lady Evelyn had come round but shakily held a handkerchief to her mouth.

Johnny noticed Mr Merryweather sniffing the air and frowning. 'What about the smell of perfume?' asked Johnny.

Everyone looked at him blankly, except for Mr Merryweather, who tilted his head.

'Let us quickly continue,' insisted Howard Carter, who shone a large torch inside. Everyone gasped as the beam of light picked out gold and ebony couches, thrones, vases and statues. At the far end was another set of doors between a pair of identical statues.

'They are sculptures of Tutankhamun,' cheered Howard Carter. 'The doors to his burial chamber are intact. Gentlemen, we may be the first people to look upon the Pharaoh's sarcophagus.' He stepped between golden bowls and trumpets strewn across the floor and, once again, chiselled at the mortar between the two doors.

Mr Merryweather gestured for Johnny and Ted to follow the others as they stepped through the treasure trove. 'The curse is just a myth, but I would like to find out more about that spectral wind and the hint of, what would you say the perfume was Johnny, cedarwood perhaps?'

With a shout of triumph, Howard Carter pushed open another set of doors in the far wall.

Johnny and Ted stopped in shock. They were face-to-face with the golden mask of Tutankhamun.

'Unbelievable,' said Ted, wiping away a tear.

'It isn't here.' Mr Merryweather looked around the burial chamber. 'Well boys, we must be getting you home.'

'But,' stammered Ted, his face creased in

anguish. 'We can't leave now.'

'What isn't here?' Johnny was getting annoyed at how often the Curator hinted at things without explaining them.

'All in good time, Jonathon.' He put his finger to his lips. 'Carter, we will leave you to your inspection.'

Mr Merryweather bid everyone a good day and led Johnny and Ted from the tomb. They strode back towards the tent, where Mr Merryweather bowed curtly at Miss Price as he hurried by, ignoring her questions about when the tomb would be opened, and they were soon back in the Time Machine. He turned over the hourglass and moved the levers attached to the globe until the display showed the letters N-O-W. The room once again hummed and shook as the globe transformed into the swirling pattern of yellow and red clouds that coalesced into a twisting orange ball of light. A piece of plaster fell from the ceiling and landed on Mr Merryweather's shoulder. He briefly looked surprised, harrumphed, and then brushed it off.

'We should return to our time a mere five minutes after we departed,' smiled Mr Merryweather. 'I think we have one question answered but a mystery to solve. I believe, Jonathon, that you were the only other person to smell what I think is an old aftershave.'

Johnny nodded. 'It reminds me of something.' He wanted to ask Mr Merryweather what he meant, but as the Time Machine fell silent and the globe became still, he realised someone else was in the room.

Ted nervously nudged Johnny. 'Erm, there's something you should know.'

9

The Unexpected Burglar

'What is the meaning of this?' scolded Mr Merryweather.

Johnny's insides turned to jelly when he spotted Yaz, emerging from behind the grandfather clock, looking shocked and confused.

'What did I see out there?'

Johnny stormed over to Yaz, his face hot with anger. 'What are you doing here, Yaz? Why do you always have to spoil things?'

Mr Merryweather walked over to stand between them. 'This is rather unfortunate. I gather you two know each other. Tell me, how did you gain entry into the museum and this room?'

Yaz looked embarrassed. 'Our school is closed today for teacher training.'

Johnny glared at her. Why hadn't she told him that at breakfast?

'I'm sorry, I wanted to find out about the

museum. So I hung around out of sight for a while after the crossing then I followed you and hid in one of the big gardens over the road. I waited for a while, then I tried the door, but it was locked, and I nearly gave up when I saw an upstairs window was open.'

Mr Merryweather tutted to himself. 'Carry on.'

Yaz hesitated and took a deep breath as if she was summoning the courage to tell them more. 'You won't tell the police or my parents, will you?'

'Why not?' shouted Johnny.

'Please calm down Jonathon, let us discover what your friend has to say.' Mr Merryweather spoke quietly. 'Please continue Yaz, short for Yasmin, I presume. I give my word I shall inform neither the police nor your parents. What did you do next?'

'I climbed up a drainpipe, squeezed through the window and found the others. They said you'd come down this way, so I tried to find you. I'm sorry sir, I just didn't want to miss out.' Yaz sobbed the last few words.

'Oh do not worry, I promise you are not in trouble.' Mr Merryweather sounded irritated. 'However, I do need to know how you managed this, please.' Mr Merryweather forced a smile as he finished speaking. Johnny could see Yaz struggling to keep control as she sighed and wiped away a tear with her sleeve.

'It's a lot bigger than I thought,' she sniffed

'Indeed, carry on,' urged Mr Merryweather.

'I'd almost given up when I heard this strange buzzing sort of sound and saw the orange light below the door so I thought you'd be here. I moved the hands of the clock, I don't know why, it looked like a handle I guess. The door swung right open, so I came in. I opened the curtains and saw you all walking this way across what looked like a desert. I'm really, really sorry, I just wanted to see Museum Club for myself. I'm not even sure what made me do it.' At last, Yaz stopped talking and looked at her feet.

Mr Merryweather clasped his hands behind his back and paced around the room, muttering to himself. Johnny could hear snatches — 'serious breach of security' — 'must not happen again' — 'who else could circumvent our defences?'

The Curator seemed to have forgotten about them, so Johnny turned on Yaz, his hands balled into fists by his sides as he screamed, 'Can't you just leave me alone for once, Yaz?'

Yaz sniffed and more tears filled her eyes.

Johnny felt his anger grow hot. 'What if mum stops me? You better not tell her, right?'

He stormed off to another corner of the room and slumped to the floor with his back against the wall. His face felt hot and damp, and he realised he was crying. He wiped away tears and heard Yaz say 'no' quietly, but couldn't bear to look up at her. He jumped when the Curator slammed his hand on the table and shouted, 'By Jove, I have it!'

Johnny looked up to see Ted quaking and Yaz with her head in her hands. Mr Merryweather was, surprisingly, smiling.

'Everybody fine? Good, good. We will show Yasmin the Buxton Room.' Mr Merryweather clapped his hands. He ushered Ted and Yaz towards the door, then stood over Johnny and thrust a hand down to him. 'Up you come, Jonathon. It may appear to complicate matters, however, I think we may find this to our advantage.'

Johnny reluctantly reached up to take Mr Merryweather's hand and allowed himself to be hauled to his feet.

Once again Johnny and Ted trotted behind Mr Merryweather as he dashed along the corridors, speaking continuously. 'First, let me tell you, Yasmin, that your escapade is not only against the law but also reckless, dangerous and risked causing more damage to this museum than you could ever be aware of.'

Mr Merryweather paused for breath, one finger in the air. 'However, it was also brilliant and perfectly executed. I do not know how you pulled it off, but it demonstrates that you might be just the person we require for our mission, once you have tried the marmalade of course!'

Johnny scratched his head. How come the Curator had suddenly changed his mood, what was this about a mission and was it anything to do with the jewel-encrusted gold shield he'd shown them? Yaz was wiping away tears and, almost, managed a smile, while Ted still looked too dumbstruck to speak.

'What do you mean?' asked Johnny.

'I mean,' Mr Merryweather glanced at him over his shoulder, 'our quest to save the world, mend time and stop the barrier between our world and that of the Shadow Lord from being ripped down, torn apart and broken through.'

The Curator suddenly stopped to turn around, and they just managed not to run into him. 'Perhaps I need to explain the situation a little more. Follow me. Yasmin, you really must try some of my marmalade.'

Johnny felt more confused than ever, and very frustrated, as they resumed following the Curator through the museum. Why didn't Mr Merryweather just get on with it and tell them what this was all about?

'What is it with the marmalade?' Johnny still couldn't see what the point of it was.

'Ah, a marmalade recipe passed down the

centuries from an alchemist at the court of Queen Elizabeth. It binds with the atoms of some people to enable them to travel in time. Like little cushions, the marmalade protects you from the blow of temporal displacement. Ingenious really!'

'And who is this Shadow Lord, Mr Merryweather?' Johnny felt he had a lot of new stuff to work out — time travel, other dimensions, an evil Shadow Lord and quantum thingies. He just wanted the Curator to tell them everything.

'In good time, Jonathon,' said the Curator as he waved them on. 'Let us return to the Buxton Room first.'

'Stop!' shouted Ted. Ted never shouted. 'There's a photo of someone who looks like you. He's with Miss Price and the girl and boy we met at Tutankhamun's tomb in 1922. That is you, isn't it?'

'How did you find that photograph, Edward?' Mr Merryweather puffed out his cheeks.

'It is, isn't it?' Ted glowered at the Curator.

'Yes, you are correct.'

'But,' Ted continued, 'they didn't have their photo taken with you, did they? We did.'

Mr Merryweather nodded.

'Then let's see it.'

'Right, but we must be quick.' Mr Merryweather dashed along another corridor and once again they ran in his wake. Johnny was starting to wonder what was up with the Curator that he could move so fast for an old man. Eventually, they came to the room of Egyptian scrolls that Johnny and Ted had found on their first day.

Ted went in and flicked through the photographs of the excavation until he stopped and let out his breath. 'Impossible.' He held the photo up for them to see. There was Mr Merryweather, dressed in the same clothes he wore now and they were on either side of him dressed in the old school blazers. The old car and camels were in the background.

'What's this all about?' Yaz sounded almost scared.

'I will explain in the Buxton Room. I know a shortcut.' Mr Merryweather led them to the rear of the room, through a door and they somehow emerged into the room with the marmalade-making machine. The room was buzzing with conversation. Everyone else was already there, sitting around one of the tables eating scones with jam and cream. Johnny glanced at the large clock and was stunned to see less than twenty minutes had passed since they'd gone to the Time Machine, despite it feeling like they'd spent over an hour in 1922. Emily and Alisha looked up and whispered to each other.

'Please.' Mr Merryweather directed them to a table further away from the others, which was, surprisingly, laid for four people with plates, cups and saucers, a pot of tea and a full toast rack.

'Before we proceed, Yasmin, please help yourself to tea, toast and marmalade. It is the least I can offer. You too Jonathon and Edward, it helps ease you back into our own time. I insist.'

Yaz suspiciously picked up a slice of toast from the rack and began scraping marmalade on it as thinly as possible. The Curator snatched the knife from her hand, dipped it in the marmalade jar, and spread a thick dollop onto her toast.

'Eat this or I might change my mind about calling the police. Now, everyone, sit down.' The Curator began pacing around the tables with his hands behind his back, which made Johnny nervous, so he poured four cups of tea and reached for the toast. At last, Mr Merryweather stopped and turned towards them. Johnny chewed a mouthful of toast in expectation of finding out some answers at last.

10

The Shield and the Shadow Lord

'Jonathon, Edward.' Mr Merryweather looked at them in turn over the top of his glasses. 'You have both passed the marmalade test and successfully travelled in time. The photo is proof of that. More importantly, you have also returned to our own time. Very few people can manage this.'

Yaz paused with her half-eaten slice of toast partway to her open mouth, a dollop of marmalade about to slip off one end.

'Yasmin, you must eat more marmalade so we can test you for time-travelling abilities. I hope you pass, as you clearly have skills in breaking through the highest quantum security system without detection, skills that bode well.'

'Time travel? Quantum what?' mouthed Yaz to Johnny.

Johnny was struggling to understand anything the Curator was going on about. He got the bit about time travel and changing history from sci-fi movies, but he couldn't believe they'd just done it and he was totally lost with all the stuff about quantum security. Ted got it, he was nodding, but Yaz went back to quietly munching her toast and sniffed.

Mr Merryweather took off his glasses and rubbed them with a handkerchief he took from the top pocket of his jacket with a flourish. 'I do apologise, I am sure that this is making very little sense. Let me begin again. You remember the Shield of Ages?'

Johnny and Ted nodded.

'As I mentioned, the Shield is no ordinary historical treasure but is, what we call, a quantum vortex. It is where time and space meet in quite an exciting way.' Mr Merryweather paused. 'Do any of you know what quantum means?'

Johnny and Yaz shook their heads but Ted snapped out of his trance. 'A quantum is the smallest particle of matter or energy found inside atoms. Electrons and protons are quantum particles.'

'Erm, we've not done this in science, have we?' Johnny was sure he would have remembered it if they had.

'No.' Ted looked sheepish. 'I just like science.'

'Exactly right Edward. A quantum vortex sucks these particles together with such force that the usual rules of how the universe works are twisted out of all recognition. Most of these vortexes are natural, such as black holes and wormholes in space, but the Shield is the greatest of human inventions. It was made thousands of years ago by a lost civilisation as defence against a powerful force that was destroying cities, mountains, even whole islands. They thought this force was an evil demon, whom they called the Shadow Lord because of the void of nothingness it left behind. Their priests were the first to study stars, planets and the tiniest elements of which everything is made, what we now call atoms and particles. One priest discovered that the Shadow Lord was attacking from another world similar to ours, but that a boundary between the worlds was keeping the demon from invading. She was the first person to identify a parallel universe! That was over 10,000 years ago.'

Ted snorted in disbelief.

'Unbelievable, I know Edward, such skill.' Mr Merryweather's eyes shone. 'She calculated that the boundary was weakening under the Shadow Lord's attacks and that a defensive weapon was needed to harness sub-atomic energy and rebuild the barrier between the two worlds. They raced against time to forge a shield of twelve quantum conductors, each made from the strongest and most precious metals and minerals they knew. They set the conductors in a circle to form the vortex and, so, the Shield or was born.

'It successfully locked the boundary between dimensions but, in doing so, it created a storm of violent earthquakes, volcanoes and tsunamis that sank their city below the waves.'

'Hang on, hang on, hang on!' interrupted Ted. 'You're not trying to claim it was Atlantis, are you?'

'Indeed I am, Edward.'

'Wow,' said Johnny. He'd watched loads of programmes about Atlantis. 'That's, like, a super ancient civilisation out in the Atlantic Ocean somewhere.'

'It's just a myth.' Ted crossed his arms and sat back in his chair.

'I know this seems fantastical, and the idea of its location is mostly nonsense. Explorers have been looking in the wrong place for centuries, for which we are indebted to the subterfuge of good old Plato. The real Atlantis was a great African island city. Remains of it may still survive under thick lava fields on the Canary Islands.

'One family acted quickly as the city sank. They rescued the Shield and escaped to the African mainland. Nothing was heard of the Shield again.' Mr Merryweather drew breath.

'About the time Elizabeth I became Queen of England, inexplicable events started to occur. Whole

ed, islands crumbled into the
ical sea monsters attacked ships.
ada was sunk by a mysterious
ot be explained.'

ss sake,' exclaimed Ted.

'Please hear me out, Edward,' said Mr Merryweather. 'Two members of Elizabeth's court learnt the story of the Shield. John Blanke, a musician from Africa, and John Dee, who was an alchemist. They were translating an ancient book written in an obscure language that had been in Blanke's family for generations. The book was an account of the Shield, which Dee recognised as a treasure he was studying in the royal treasury. They realised that the strange events were caused by the Shadow Lord and the boundary between worlds must be weakening. When Dee tried various alchemical and magnetic experiments to restart the Shield nothing happened. Blanke reread the description of the Shield in the book and discovered that what they had was just a hollow vessel missing its vital components; there were spaces where the conductors should have been. They identified these as symbols of great civilisations and surmised that they must have been scattered around the world long before their own time. Blanke and Dee swore an oath to reunite the objects, what we now call conductors, with the Shield and they created this museum as its first curators. I too have taken that oath. For five hundred years, the museum's curators have searched for the conductors, helped more recently by the Time Machine of Mr Wells.

'So far we have retrieved six quantum conductors, we are halfway there. But the Shadow Lord has recently become aware of our work and is racing us for the remaining lost conductors. He only needs to find one to stop the Shield working.'

Alisha came over to ask what they should do next and Mr Merryweather went over to talk to them. Johnny realised he'd been leaning forward, a slice of cold toast squashed into one hand, his jaw sore from concentration. He relaxed back into his chair and breathed out. Had he even taken a breath while Mr Merryweather had been speaking?

When Mr Merryweather returned, he took out the small silver egg and passed it backwards and forwards in front of Yaz. It hummed to itself, lit up with a green light and made a satisfied sounding beep.

'Excellent,' enthused Mr Merryweather.

'What's that?' asked Yaz.

'This little scanner shows whether the marmalade will successfully protect your atoms during time travel. They all need to appear in the same place, at the same time, otherwise, bits of you risk being taken to different periods, which can be very messy.'

'Urgh, that's gross,' exclaimed Yaz.

'That is not the worst thing that can happen,' replied Mr Merryweather.

'And,' asked Ted, slowly, 'what is worse than that?'

'Ending up in Nowhere, Edward. For eternity. Let us not dwell on this, however. The marmalade works on you all, which means time travel with hardly any risks.'

'This Shadow Lord,' Yaz was frowning, 'is he, like, real?'

'Indeed he is,' replied Mr Merryweather.

Ted snorted in disbelief. 'What does this Shadow Lord look like then?'

'Also a good question Edward. He has always worked by controlling elements in our dimension. No one has seen him because he has never been able to enter our world from his own.'

'Convenient,' retorted Ted.

Mr Merryweather ignored him. 'However, I believe that he has captured a person from our world, who he has disassembled into an atomic entity of great power. He is using this 'puppet' to seek out the Shield's quantum conductors. If the Shadow Lord can destroy just one conductor, then the Shield will never be complete and the barrier will grow weaker and weaker until he can invade our universe to unleash a reign of terror.'

Johnny started to shake. 'Was that the thing that attacked me at the start of term?'

'Tell me more Johnny.' Mr Merryweather looked pale and had lost the twinkle in his eyes.

Johnny told the Curator what had happened the morning he'd ended up in Mr Everard's rose bushes, including getting pins and needles, becoming angry and then the thing disappearing. As he spoke, Johnny felt more and more sure it must have been the Shadow Lord. Ted held his head in his hands.

'Mr Everard has been to tell me about this, but he wasn't sure what he had seen. He was a researcher at the museum many years ago until he retired due to his nerves. He claimed that there was too much history and it wouldn't stop doing things.' Mr Merryweather turned to Ted. 'Edward, were you there?'

'Yes, but nothing happened, Johnny just had a fight with Jordan and lost his trainer.' Ted looked as sceptical as he could manage.

'But we never did find Johnny's trainer,' said Yaz, her voice trembling.

The Curator began pacing again. 'This confirms everything. I am sure that whatever attacked you and the "warm wind" that escaped from Tutankhamun's tomb are one and the same thing, the person from our world that the Shadow Lord controls. This also means that he can move him or her through time to a certain extent.

'I don't think you had pins and needles from a dead arm or that the Shadow Lord let you go of his own free will. I believe you fought back with powers you aren't yet aware of.'

Johnny felt dumbstruck. This was getting way crazier. Was Mr Merryweather talking superhero powers, magic, or some weirdy science? Ted and Yaz stared at him.

'Do not look so alarmed Jonathon. We all have the ability to control atomic particles to a certain extent, most people just don't know how to. Those who can rarely understand what they are doing. They have been called many things over the centuries — wizards, witches, yogis, shamen, seers, alchemists, charlatans, geniuses. Yasmin, I believe you also have this ability, that's the only explanation for how you broke in. Edward, you too can work with quantum forces, if only you learn to be less sceptical.'

'Quantum mechanics? No one has the science to use it,' Ted spluttered.

'Let us just say the technology is a little bit secret.' Mr Merryweather chuckled. 'There is a school, very different to any you know, that can teach all of you how to use your skills. But first, we must discover more about the Shadow Lord. I would like you to join the museum's mission to make the Shield of Ages complete once again. We can re-energise its powers and prevent the Shadow Lord from ever reaching our world!'

'Like how?' laughed Yaz. 'We're just a bunch of kids.'

'Children you may be, ineffectual you are not.'

Johnny realised they'd been looking for the lost parts of the Shield in the museum's collection. 'So, where do we find them?'

'Not just where, Jonathon, but when!' The Curator's eyes twinkled once again. 'We found four conductors during the museum's first four hundred years, through travelling the world to collect them. That was hard and time-consuming. The other two have been traced using the Time Machine within the last century. I now believe the best way to locate them is to go back in time to when the conductors were being used by the different civilisations that, let's say, acquired them in the centuries after Atlantis was destroyed. The Time Machine has a range of 5,000 years, which means we cannot travel to the time when the Shield was still whole. Talking of time, I am afraid it has defeated us for today. That must wait until next week.'

Johnny and Yaz groaned in exasperation.

'I understand your eagerness. However, I need

to make a few more, minor, calculations to precisely locate a conductor I feel I am close to. Hurry, please. Your school will not tolerate you all returning late. No one at the school must try to close down the Club and jeopardise our mission.'

11

Ancient Egyptian Mission Impossible?

It had been two long, frustrating weeks for Johnny, Ted and Yaz since they had heard about the mission before Mr Merryweather spoke to them about it again. The Curator helped Yaz get special permission from her school to join them at Museum Club and her parents were delighted she was doing High School stuff already.

They met in the Egyptian Gallery, where they had heard the strange knocking a few weeks ago. Johnny was still convinced it had come from one of the mummies, and he tried to frighten Yaz by telling her what had happened.

'Cool,' said Yaz, 'a haunted museum. Be great to spend the night here.'

Yaz was so annoying at times, thought Johnny.

'Don't,' whispered Ted, staring nervously at the

mummies. 'The Curator explained it was just old water pipes.'

'You didn't seem so sure then,' said Johnny tapping Ted's shoulder.

'Stop it,' exclaimed Ted, as he jumped with fright.

'Have you found any of Pharaoh Ay's secrets yet Edward?' Mr Merryweather rubbed his hand across the head of the sarcophagus. 'I am sure he is the key to finding the Golden Ankh of Thebes. It was a symbol of life for the Pharaohs but the only definite record we, that is I, have found that refers to it dates to the reign of Tutankhamun, hence our little trip to see Howard Carter. It wasn't buried in his tomb, so we must visit him when he was still alive.'

'What, actually go to Ancient Egypt?' Ted's eyes widened.

Mr Merryweather nodded.

'Ted! I thought you said time travel was rubbish?' Johnny grinned at his friend.

Ted held his head high. 'I've reconciled myself to it.'

Johnny put his hands on his hips and grinned even more. 'Ooh, you've reconciled yourself, have you?'

Mr Merryweather put his hand up. 'Edward, I believe you will relish the opportunity to experience Egypt at the time of the New Kingdom. Watch out for Ay, he will be a threat to your mission.'

'Will we meet him or Tutankhamun?' asked Johnny.

'Almost certainly, though hopefully not on your first expedition. This will be a brief mission simply to familiarise yourselves with Thebes and test the language translators.'

'I've been on holiday there,' said Ted. 'It's called Luxor now.'

'Great, you can show us around,' said Johnny. 'When do we go?'

'Well, I thought now would be as good a time as any,' replied Mr Merryweather.

'Now?' Johnny, Ted and Yaz shouted in unison.

'I really can't be late for tea if my mum's going to allow me to come back,' said Johnny.

Mr Merryweather reached into his jacket pocket and took out a polished wooden box with brass fittings. 'No need to worry about that Jonathon. You see, we benefit from time dilation. First, I'd like you each to have a translator.'

The Curator examined three small, oval capsules cradled in red velvet inside the box. Each appeared to be made of glass and was full of a swirling cloud of orange gas similar to the Time Machine's globe.

Yaz sighed in exasperation. 'What is time dilation exactly?'

'I'll use the translators to explain,' said Mr

Merryweather. 'If you pop one into your right ear you will understand any language, in any time period, and anything you say will be automatically translated into that language. Ingenious little things.' He passed them each a capsule.

Johnny looked at Ted and Yaz looked at Johnny, and they each pressed a capsule into their ear. Johnny felt it buzz and tingle as it slid in.

'Weird, totally weird,' shouted Yaz, scrabbling at her ear. 'Make it … stop … oh, it has.'

Ted dug a finger into his ear. 'It tickles.' The translator popped out and Ted studied it.

'They are some of the latest quantum technology, self-charging as you move and one-hundred per cent accurate. You will return them to me after the mission.'

Ted put the translator back in his ear.

'Can you all understand my Serbo-Croat, Swahili or Samoan?' asked the Curator.

'That's just English,' scowled Yaz.

Mr Merryweather moved something in the box. 'I've made a little adjustment to the operating system. How is my Hungarian? Let me say this in Hindi. Still, understanding what I say? Perhaps there is a slight tingle at the start of every sentence, as the translator recalibrates for the different languages. How is Navajo or Greenland Inuit?'

Johnny looked at Yaz in surprise. He could hear

one different language after another but could understand it as if Mr Merryweather was speaking English inside his head.

'Who knows French?' asked Mr Merryweather.

Ted put his hand up.

'Good, say something in French.'

Ted asked a long rambling question about how to get to the station. Johnny could sort of hear him speak French but the words seemed to just pop into his head in English.

'OK, these are officially cool,' said Yaz.

'Very good,' said Mr Merryweather. 'Now let me speak in Japanese to explain our old friend time dilation. It all comes down to Albert Einstein, a genius who was extraordinarily helpful in repairing the Time Machine. His Theory of Relativity showed how time slows down the further away you are from your point of origin. An astronaut travelling to our nearest star and back at the speed of light would be only 8.7 years older by the time he returned, yet 120 years would have passed on Earth! Einstein did not realise, until we found out by trial and error, that this also applies to time travel — but in reverse! As a result, whenever you go back in time, only one hour passes in the present for every day you spend in the past. This is very convenient, as I'm sure you agree.'

'We can still be home for tea?' asked Johnny.

'Absolutely.'

'We could do a lot in that time,' said Johnny.

'Indeed you can. I propose you are away for a maximum of ten minutes of our time, which gives you four hours in Thebes. Nothing adventurous of course, just have a brief stroll around, find the temple and have a go at talking to some of the inhabitants. How does that sound?'

Johnny suddenly realised it was for real. 'Hang on, aren't you coming?'

'I'm afraid this old body is no longer fit enough to travel more than about two hundred years into the past.'

'Erm, don't we need longer?' asked Ted. 'To, you know, prepare?'

'Let's do it,' said Yaz, as she leapt to her feet.

They went straight to the Time Machine. Johnny felt even more excited as soon as they were inside. He could tell Ted and Yaz felt the same.

'There are a few things that you should know.' Mr Merryweather opened a cupboard packed full of jars of his homemade marmalade stacked on top of each other. 'Remember to eat plenty when you return home. While I hope you do not pick up an injury, if you do, the large green box in the corner can mend anything from a bee sting to a broken leg. That reminds me, first aid training would have been useful. Maybe next time.'

Mr Merryweather moved over to the wardrobe and flung open the doors. It was full of off-white skirts, kilts, tunics, shirts and dresses.

'There is everything from slave to aristocrat. I recommend dressing down to attract less attention,' said Mr Merryweather, handing them each a set of rough, grubby tunics.

'Oh, one more thing,' said the Curator, pointing to the grandfather clock. One set of hands pointed to twenty past ten, another pair to twenty past twelve and the third pair of hands to twenty-past six. 'Keep an eye on this clock, which always tells you the time now at home, your time at your destination and the time in Lhasa, Tibet. I still don't know why it tells the time in Tibet, but it does. Remember one thing, do not be late.'

'Everyone happy?' The Curator looked around and Johnny nodded enthusiastically. 'In that case, there is no time to lose. I will start you on your way. Remember what the Time Machine looks like, where it is and head straight back to it if you encounter any trouble.'

Ted put his hand up. 'I'm having second thoughts about this.'

'You don't have to go if you don't want to, Edward.' Mr Merryweather smiled gently.

'Come on Ted,' said Yaz, nudging him. 'We'll get to meet some of these old Egyptian characters and check out the shops.'

'It sounds fun and we'll stay close to the Time Machine, to begin with.' Johnny surprised himself with how confident he sounded.

'Yes, OK,' said Ted quietly.

They gathered around the globe and Mr Merryweather once again pulled levers, pushed buttons and flipped over the hourglass. The room started to hum and shake and the map of the world faded to the swirling mass of red and yellow clouds.

'Everything is set for the year Tutankhamun becomes Pharaoh, 1332 BC in our calendar. Time for me to leave. I now bid you farewell, good luck and bon voyage. See you in ten minutes or so.'

Mr Merryweather quickly left the room and they were alone. Almost instantly, he dashed back in, startling them all. 'I nearly forgot! When you need to return to our time simply press this.' He pointed to a large, red button hidden underneath the rim. The word 'HOME' was engraved on a brass plaque beside the button. 'It is much easier than fiddling around with the levers. Bon voyage!'

Mr Merryweather slammed the door as he sprinted through it. They sat down in the red leather armchairs arranged around the globe and watched its red and yellow clouds glow brighter and swirl faster as they mixed to golden orange. The Time Machine hummed, rattled and shook as the N-O-W numerals on the rim of the globe clicked over, each flipping faster and faster until they were all a blur. The tick-tock of the grandfather clock echoed around the room, while its hands spun so fast they were invisible.

12

Street Gang of Ancient Egypt

The Time Machine slowly shuddered to a silent halt. Johnny, Ted and Yaz unpeeled themselves from the armchairs and went to change into their Egyptian clothes. Johnny noticed the counters on the globe no longer gave the date in Roman numerals but were replaced by hieroglyphs. He looked at the clock, the hands of all three pairs of hands had moved on by a minute.

First Johnny, then Yaz, and finally, cautiously, Ted, poked their heads out of the Time Machine door.

The heat hit them instantly, like a thousand hair dryers on full blast. It was the same hard, scorching heat and blindingly bright sun that had welcomed them to Egypt in 1922.

'I wish I had my shades.' Yaz squinted up and down the street.

'Bit of a giveaway,' said Ted smugly. 'They

hadn't been invented 3,000 years ago.'

'You might be right, but that doesn't stop you from being a pain,' replied Yaz.

'OK you two, cut it out.' Johnny felt they needed to stick together to survive Ancient Egypt, even for a couple of hours. Meeting Howard Carter with Mr Merryweather was one thing, but Ancient Egypt on their own felt very different. He took a deep breath, shaded his eyes with his hand, and stepped outside.

They were in a straight, sandy street between low, earth-coloured buildings with red-tiled roofs. There were a few, small shuttered windows in the walls of the buildings. It was silent and appeared to be empty, which was a relief.

'From the position of the sun, I reckon the clock's right, it's about midday,' said Ted. 'Hopefully, Ancient Egyptians have a siesta and we can have a look around before we need to speak to anyone.'

'I hope we don't meet anybody. I wouldn't want to be seen dead in these clothes,' replied Yaz.

The rough, grubby tunics made them itch and the papyrus sandals were already chafing Johnny's feet, but he was glad not to be walking barefoot on hot sand and stones.

'Let's make sure we know where's the Time Machine and what it looks like!' called Ted.

They turned around and saw a run-down, ramshackle house, just like the others on the street, with a small shuttered window high-up under the roof and a plank door that had a heavy wooden handle and lock. The plaster was falling off, leaving big gaps where red clay and brown reeds showed through.

'Come on,' said Johnny and headed for the corner of the street, followed closely by Yaz and Ted. Within seconds Johnny felt his skin prickle with sweat.

The sight they saw around the corner stopped them all in their tracks. Towering three or four times higher than the houses was a massive building with huge, brightly painted columns topped by a wall of thick stone slabs. It was completely covered in colourful patterns and pictures of gods and pharaohs.

'Wow, it's beautiful,' said Yaz.

'Is that the temple?' asked Johnny. The street went straight up to one end of the building and he set off towards it. He didn't like stopping for too long in case he thought too much about where — and when — they were.

Ted filled them in with what he knew. 'Luxor Temple, dedicated to the king of the gods. What I remember from our holiday were massive statues of Pharaoh Rameses the Second by a big door on the end of the temple.'

Johnny closed and opened his eyes, just to make

sure he really was looking at an Ancient Egyptian temple, then broke into a grin when it was still there. This really is real, he thought.

Ted shook his head. 'I can't believe I'm seeing this, Luxor Temple as it was.'

'As it is you mean,' said Yaz.

Ted laughed. 'Yeah, as it is. Unbelievable. Just think, we're the first people from our time to see Luxor Temple when it was new!'

Johnny felt they should move on, he was nervous about looking suspicious. 'Ted, as you've been here before, where do we go?'

'That was a long time ago,' replied Ted

'Not yet it isn't,' said Yaz.

'Where are we then?' asked Johnny, starting to feel impatient.

Ted looked around and scratched the back of his head. 'It's totally different now. The only thing I recognise is the temple. This is one of its long sides, which must mean the Nile is on the other side. If we want to look around we can walk to the far end of the temple and find the entrance.'

'I'm going to, the pictures are pretty wacky,' said Yaz as she set off.

'Hieroglyphs,' called Ted after her. 'They're words.'

They walked along the temple wall for what seemed like ages, the heat making them sweat until they reached a corner. They could see the Nile shimmering beyond a long avenue of lion-like stone sphinxes. Johnny wanted to stand by the river, so he led them between the sphinxes, where he instinctively looked left and right to cross the avenue. He stopped to stare as he saw the magnificent entrance to the temple. A huge gate was set in another high wall, painted with hundreds of rows of hieroglyphs and giant pictures of archers riding chariots. In front of the wall stood six giant stone sculptures of Pharaohs with bare chests, white loincloths and blue and white striped Egyptian headdresses, topped with red and white crowns. Each statue was painted with skin, eyes and eyebrows; their ribs and muscles were carved into the stone and they looked as lifelike as possible for huge sculptures. The largest two figures sat on either side of the immense doorway.

'No way,' said Ted. 'They're the statues of Rameses.'

They were startled when a man with a shaved ran out of the temple, shouting at them to "stop."

'Let's go,' said Ted, turning back the way they'd come.

Johnny grabbed him by the arm. 'Quick, make a run for it. I want to see the Nile.'

Johnny dragged Ted across the avenue, Yaz following close behind. The guard-priest shouted angrily but he didn't look like he was about to run after them and they were soon lost in a maze of little lanes winding between more ramshackle wooden buildings. The overpowering smell of fish made Johnny feel a bit sick and he was relieved to come out from between the huts and reach the open air by the Nile.

They sheltered under the shade of a palm tree to watch boats sail down the middle of the river, each piled high with large bales of cotton. Men and boys were working on a group of moored boats, coiling ropes, repairing fishing nets and sails, or loading clay jars and more cloth bales. No one gave them a second glance. Johnny's heart stirred, he was standing beside the Nile, something he'd never dreamt he'd do.

A large group of laughing, shouting children tumbled out of the narrow alleys towards them. It looked like they were playing a chaotic game with a ball and curved sticks.

'Hockey?' said Yaz, quizzically.

As one, the group stopped, fell silent and stared. Johnny thought the children looked about two or three years younger than them.

'Uh-oh,' said Ted quietly as he backed behind Yaz. She took up the jujitsu fighting stance with one foot in front of the other, her knees slightly bent and her hands outstretched flat with her fingertips pointing towards the children. Ted bumped into the palm tree behind him and Johnny couldn't suppress a giggle.

The tallest boy in the gang pushed through the others to stand in front of Yaz, his hands on his hips. 'Ah, you want to wrestle. A challenge I accept.'

He stepped forward in a low crouch, his arms outstretched, and began to circle Yaz, who constantly turned to face him.

'Wow, we really can understand them,' whispered Ted.

Johnny nodded but kept his gaze firmly on Yaz and the boy. He didn't want them to get into a fight in case losing a wrestling match would lead to anything that would stop them returning to the Time Machine.

With a shriek, the boy lunged at Yaz, coming at her at a low angle and aiming for her stomach. Yaz stepped to one side, turned with him, trapped his arm under hers and stood up. Suddenly, he was screeching in pain while trying to balance on the tips of his toes.

'Let me go, let me go,' he howled.

The rest of his gang were laughing and shouting, and Johnny could pick out snatches of what they said — 'she beat Ipi' — 'best of three' — 'what happened Ipi?' They seemed to think the whole thing was a big joke.

'Why did you attack us?' Yaz slowly turned around, and the boy had to follow to stop his arm from snapping.

'Yaz!' called Johnny. 'I think it's a game.'

The boy nodded, his face screwed up in pain, sweat now dripping from his forehead.

Ted groaned. 'Of course, wrestling is big among Egyptian children.'

Yaz sighed and released the pressure on the boy's arm, but she stared at him warily just in case he was pretending and tried to attack again.

Ipi sat down, rubbed his arm and scowled at Yaz. 'Strange technique Assyrian, but we always not hurt each other.'

'Best of three, best of three,' chanted the other children in the gang.

Ipi shook his head. 'I do not want to wrestle the Assyrian again.'

'I'm not Syrian,' Yaz pouted. 'My dad's from Bangladesh and mum's from Lewisham.'

The Egyptian children all looked at her blankly. Johnny wondered if the translators had stopped working until one of the girls ran up, touched Ted's arm and called. 'You're it, Nubian!'

'Don't let the Greek boy catch you or he'll give you the plague,' shouted another girl.

The rest of the gang shouted 'urgh' and quickly scattered down the alleys.

'Now what?' Johnny looked around.

'Chase after them of course,' replied Yaz, heading towards the nearest alley.

Johnny grinned and followed her.

'We shouldn't do this,' Ted called after them.

13

Tea with Tutankhamun and the Riddle of the Sphinx

The narrow alley sliced between two rows of buildings with roofs of reeds that touched above their heads, instantly plunging them into darkness. Fishbones lay scattered on the sand, swept up into small dunes against the cracked and dirty walls. The alley snaked between buildings and Johnny tried to keep up with Yaz as she constantly disappeared and reappeared ahead of him. Johnny could hear Ted breathing heavily behind him. They occasionally passed small, dark doorways with only thick blankets as curtain doors and even narrower alleyways that crisscrossed from one side to the other.

Yaz halted at a crossroads and Johnny caught up with her. 'Where did they go?' He peered in each direction, but there was no sign of the gang.

'No idea,' said Yaz. 'Time to go?'

'Yes!' pleaded Ted, who wriggled his way between Johnny and Yaz.

They hurried back down the alleyway, trying to find the river again by retracing their steps. Soon they were completely lost in the maze of narrow, dark lanes.

'Where are we?' Ted's voice quavered as he stopped.

'Oh, get a grip, Ted,' said Yaz impatiently. 'There's always a way out.'

'Of course there is.' The man with the shaved head who had shouted from the temple stepped in front of them, backed up by three guards. He had black eye make-up and expensive-looking clothes, and he was brandishing a scroll.

Johnny thought he recognised him from the museum. He was about to turn and run when the man's harsh voice stopped him in his tracks. 'You have been chosen to take milk and wine with our glorious Pharaoh Tutankhamun to celebrate the Festival of Thoth.'

'What? Do you know about this Ted?' Johnny felt like they'd won the lottery, the chance to meet Tutankhamun, but thought it must be a scam.

'Erm, no,' murmured Ted, standing behind Johnny and Yaz.

'Come, come,' replied the man, who was now

holding his nose. 'There is nothing to be afraid of. The Pharaoh has decided to invite three street children to be part of the Festival in the first year of his reign. He hopes it will become a tradition and you are honoured to be the first. Hurry up, so that I can leave this stinking dungheap — and remember to be grateful.' He turned to the men behind him. 'Guards.'

'Yes, Grand Vizier!' They stepped forward and grabbed Johnny, Ted and Yaz.

'Take them to the temple,' ordered the man. 'I do not know what the boy is thinking of. Never trust a child to be Pharaoh.'

Johnny's mind was whirring as they were led out of the alleys. The Grand Vizier was the mummy in the sarcophagus at the museum, the one Johnny was sure knocked the day Emily was sick. That's where he recognised him from, he looked just like his portrait on his sarcophagus. Johnny's mind went haywire. The dead mummy in the museum in his time was, is, the living man walking in front of them right now, thousands of years in the past, but also their current present. It was way too much to work out.

They were escorted past tall obelisks and the huge statues through the doors of Luxor Temple and into a courtyard surrounded by even more painted columns. Johnny felt they were under arrest rather than guests and wondered whether human sacrifice was a thing in Ancient Egypt. He saw a group of people at the far end of the courtyard, and in the centre was a boy younger than them sitting on a golden chair. He wore a red and white Egyptian crown and a gold-embroidered tunic. The boy looked nervous, surrounded by some very stern and important-looking men and women, but smiled when he saw them.

'Dear guests, please join me.' Tutankhamun gestured to an elaborately woven blanket in front of the throne.

That was when Johnny noticed it; the Golden Ankh was on the back of the throne! He didn't dare say anything to Ted and Yaz, he guessed talking in front of the Pharaoh might be the sort of thing you got punished for by having your head cut off or something equally gruesome. The guards marched them to the edge of the blanket.

'Sit down,' hissed the Grand Vizier. 'Keep your eyes down, and only speak when the Pharaoh talks to you.'

The guards pushed them down until they knelt, foreheads pressed to the blanket.

'Not so rough Ay,' ordered Tutankhamun. 'Please relax and excuse my Grand Vizier.'

Johnny, Ted and Yaz looked up into the kind, smiling face of the Pharaoh. Johnny had loads of questions racing around his mind and was sure Ted must have more. He also noticed the Grand Vizier had a face like thunder and was standing next to the throne, tapping the fingers of one hand on the top of the Golden Ankh. They were so close to it, but it was too heavily guarded for them to have any chance to get it, thought Johnny.

'Milk, wine and cakes.' Tutankhamun clapped his hands and three slaves came forward carrying jugs and plates stacked high with cakes dripping in honey. They each nibbled a cake and sipped the drinks, which were, thought Johnny, frankly disgusting and weird.

'As you know, today is my first Festival of Thoth,' continued Tutankhamun, 'which I intend to share with poor street children each year. What are your names?'

They each muttered their names and the Pharaoh laughed as if delighted. He asked them what games they liked to play, and Ted made something up based on what they'd just seen from the street gang. After what seemed like a short time, the Grand Vizier leant forward and whispered to Tutankhamun.

'I am afraid the boring man Ay tells me it is time to return to the palace. This means I can tell you the good news. You will become my personal slaves. We will have so much fun and you will not have to worry about your next meal ever again. You are so lucky!'

'First, a wash in the river my lord, and then they will be brought to the palace.' The Grand Vizier smiled menacingly at them.

'A good idea Ay. We will go ahead.' Tutankhamun beckoned four large slaves to him, who lifted his chair onto their shoulders and left the temple, followed by the Grand Vizier and other officials carried in smaller and less lavish chairs.

The guards pushed Johnny, Ted and Yaz between the columns towards a door. Johnny groaned. How were they going to get out of this and back to the Time Machine?

A deeply rich, man's voice called out to them from the shadows of a darkened side room. 'That will do guards. Leave the Pharaoh's new slaves here and I will take care of them.'

The guards looked at each other, shrugged and left them alone.

'In here.' The words were as thick and sweet as melting chocolate. 'Why don't you all come in?'

'I, I don't think that's wise,' trembled Ted.

'I am sure you do not want to become palace slaves.' The voice was beguiling but Johnny hesitated at the door. 'That's it, please enter if you would like to know how to find your way out.'

'Oh, for goodness sake,' exclaimed Yaz

impatiently. She marched in and took up her fighting posture. Johnny followed but Ted hung back just inside the door.

'I don't think this is wise,' said Ted.

There was a man, half in shade, half in light, at the far end of the room. He appeared to be wearing a Pharaoh's headdress. A large cat, which Johnny thought was big enough to be a lion, was stretched out in front of him.

As soon as they were all inside, the door slammed shut and the room was filled with lamplight. They all jumped backwards. Johnny stood on Ted's toes.

'Ouch!' screamed Ted.

'Ouch indeed,' purred the voice.

Johnny had to rub his eyes. What he'd thought was a person with a pet lion was the head and neck of a man on the body of a lion. Surely, real live Sphinxes didn't exist?

'I see you are impressed.' The Sphinx spoke directly to Johnny as if he read his mind. 'I do indeed exist. How do you do?'

They all stared with open mouths.

'Well, you are a quiet lot, aren't you? I am intrigued, which is why I have appeared here to meet you. I sense you do not quite belong here. Tell me more.'

'We're just street children,' said Johnny.

'Street children are common, and you look a little more unique,' replied the Sphinx in dulcet tones. He sat back on his haunches and inspected the claw of one of his front paws with feigned interest. 'Never mind, you are my prisoners now. That is unless you can solve the riddle of the Sphinx.'

'A riddle?' Ted asked cautiously.

'Yes, a riddle. Answer it correctly and you may go, but get it wrong and you're cat food.' The Sphinx meowed a laugh to himself.

Johnny pushed Ted to the front. Ted was great at cracking codes and solving logic puzzles.

'Are you ready?' The Sphinx stood up and towered above them.

Ted nodded.

'Here is your riddle. You have one chance to answer, one opportunity to win your freedom and your lives.' The Sphinx cleared his throat. Johnny got the impression the beast was doing all this for dramatic effect. Did mythical creatures do that?

'It travels on four feet in the morning,
two feet at noon, and three feet in the evening.
When it is on most feet,
it is at its weakest and slowest.
What is it?'

Johnny didn't have a clue and Yaz looked just as

flummoxed as he felt, so they stared at Ted in hope.

Ted furrowed his brows in concentration then looked astonished. 'Of course,' he exclaimed. 'I know this, this is easy.'

'Well?' The Sphinx arched an eyebrow.

'It is man, a human. First, we crawl as babies on all fours, then we walk on our two feet until we are old, when we use a stick!'

'Oh blast you! You are right. I knew I should have tried you with something a little more difficult but I am bound by convention and this riddle must always be the first I ask. I must let you go, but the next time we meet I will have a much knottier riddle for you.'

With that, the Sphinx melted into thin air, leaving a few wisps of mist behind as the door slowly opened.

'Well,' breathed Ted, 'that was frightening.'

'You did it though,' said Johnny.

'Well done, I'm impressed. Now let's get out of here before anything else weird appears.' Yaz strode past them and they were soon back in the courtyard where they had met Tutankhamun. It was strangely empty and one of the massive doors to the outside was slightly open. They slid through the gap, quickly looked around for guards, and ran back through streets, now filling with people, towards the Time Machine. It wasn't long before they were back in their own time and spreading marmalade on toast that popped out of the toaster as soon as they arrived.

'It's just half-past ten,' said Ted, shaking his head in disbelief. 'That's just ten minutes after we set off for Ancient Egypt.'

14

Return to Egypt

Johnny bounded down the stairs two steps at a time and was very early for breakfast. He'd been awake and ready for what felt like hours, keen to return to the museum and their next trip to Ancient Egypt. He threw open the kitchen door and was surprised to find Yaz already sitting at the table, with a cup of hot chocolate.

She beamed at him as he rushed in. 'Can't wait either?'

All three of them hadn't stopped talking about Tutankhamun, Ay and the Sphinx since their visit to Thebes last week.

'I've hardly slept.' He dashed over to the toaster, rammed four slices of bread into the slots and took a jar from the cupboard. 'Marmalade?'

They both laughed.

Johnny heard his mum coming down the stairs and turned to frown at the toaster as she entered. He didn't want to give her any reason to get suspicious about their visits to the museum.

'Well, it's lovely to hear you both getting on so well.' She bustled over to the kettle, filled it and dropped three teabags into the pot. 'What's the joke?'

Johnny glanced at Yaz, who stared down at her magazine.

'Come on now, I like a good laugh as much as anyone.' His mum looked quizzically at the side of the milk bottle, challenging it to still be in date. 'It isn't rude, is it?'

'Erm, it really wasn't that good mum.' Johnny went red as he tried to think of a joke, but his mind was totally blank.

'Oh, I see.' His mum sniffed the milk, decided it was good enough and poured it into her cup. 'You're both bright and early this morning. Anything special on?' She looked questioningly between them, but as they didn't answer, she continued, 'Oh, of course, Museum Club. It must be going better than expected I suppose. What do you like about it Yaz? I still can't figure out how your school has allowed you to join.'

Yaz raised her eyebrows at Johnny as if to ask for help.

'It's a transition to High School thing mum.' Johnny said the first thing that came to mind.

'That's, erm, right, Mrs Armstrong. It's like, well, I really like it, especially the, erm, the cataloguing and stuff.'

His mum frowned. 'What sort of stuff?'

Johnny stared at Yaz, hoping she wouldn't say too much while trying to arrange his face into an expression of only slight interest.

'Oh, like, you know…' Yaz glanced away.

'No, I do not know, Yasmin.'

Why was his mum being so abrupt? And with Yaz? He knew she didn't like the Curator and the museum, but she'd never really said why and had seemed happy with Museum Club.

'Well,' Yaz started again, hesitating over every word. 'We do quite a bit of dusting objects, Mrs Armstrong.'

'That doesn't sound interesting at all,' his mum interrupted. She never interrupted Yaz.

'Oh, but I've held some amazing things from, erm, Egypt and Assyria, that's it, I'm really interested in those places.'

Johnny couldn't help groaning out loud.

'Something wrong Johnny?' His mum turned on him, wielding a butter knife in his direction. What had got into her this morning?

Johnny paused. 'Nothing mum, we've just heard a lot about Egypt, haven't we Yaz? I've got a bit bored about it, that's all.'

'What? Oh yes. Egypt's interesting though,' continued Yaz.

Johnny couldn't believe Yaz was still talking about Egypt and glared at her.

'Or it was, but it's a bit boring now, definitely boring now.' Yaz nodded, smiled at his mum, and went back to reading her magazine as if nothing had happened. There was a heavy silence, only interrupted by his toast popping up.

Johnny wanted to know why his mum was so picky about the Museum Club this morning, but he also wanted to change the subject.

His mum glared at them through the steam rising from her mug of tea. 'Well, that's good then. OK you two, get a move on. I've got to work and you're so keen to get to school, or at least that museum, you may as well clear out the way.'

Johnny and Yaz leapt up together, Johnny with a handful of toast, and grabbed their bags.

'Bye mum,' he said as he disappeared through the door.

'What's bugging her?' asked Yaz.

Johnny strode on in silence. He was trying to think of anything that could have happened to make her more suspicious about the museum. He had seen her thrust a bundle of old family photos into an envelope when he popped downstairs for a drink last night. Could it be anything to do with dad?

Yaz continued, 'What's she got against the museum?'

'I don't know, she's never said,' Johnny replied gruffly, still annoyed that Yaz had mentioned Egypt. Yaz hadn't given anything away, but just saying the name out loud in front of his mum felt awkward. He didn't want her asking more questions in case they blurted something out that gave away what they'd been doing.

'Maybe we should find out?' asked Yaz.

Before he could stop himself, he shouted, 'No. Just leave it, right!' Johnny felt the anger rise inside. It felt like family stuff and he didn't want Yaz quizzing him about it. He stormed off, passing Ted without saying anything. He was even angrier with himself for losing his cool and blanking Ted. Of course, Yaz hadn't said anything that would make his mum stop them from going to the museum. There was obviously a good chance it would have Egyptian things and the Curator might just happen to talk about Ancient Egypt. It was on their curriculum for goodness sake. But, but, but! The sound of angry bees flew around his head again, but he told himself he must calm down.

* * *

Johnny, Ted and Yaz waited in the museum entrance hall while Mr Merryweather handed out tasks to the others and they headed off through different doorways. Mr Merryweather was wearing plus fours, a tank top with a diamond pattern and a very baggy flat cap.

'What's with the comical clothes?' Johnny whispered to Ted.

'Nineteen-Twenties' American playboy by the look of them,' Ted giggled.

'No time to waste today,' puffed the Curator, slightly breathless, as he rushed along the corridor to the room full of Egyptian mummies.

They went over to a table to tuck into tea, toast and marmalade. A large map of Thebes was held down by Egyptian jars, a toast rack and golf clubs. Johnny didn't want to wait a minute longer to be back in Ancient Egypt, and his mind wandered over the painted sarcophagi lined up along the wall. Johnny realised the Curator was explaining the mission to them when he heard his name.

'Did you hear any of that Jonathon?' Mr Merryweather looked over the top of his glasses.

Johnny shook his head. 'Sorry.'

'It was nothing,' sighed Yaz. 'Just the most important bit.'

'Never mind,' chuckled Mr Merryweather. 'I'm sure Edward and Yasmin will not be overly bored to listen to it all over again. You will spend two days in Thebes. You could have five days there before

Museum Club finishes for the day, but let's not take too many risks on your second journey. I do not want to have kittens at three o'clock this afternoon. This should be enough time for you to locate the Golden Ankh and return safely to the Time Machine. We can then develop a strategy to retrieve the ankh. We might even bring it home before Christmas. Just think what a present that would be.'

Johnny hung on Mr Merryweather's every word this time, the mission coming alive in his mind as the Curator pointed at various places on a map. The River Nile ran through the centre like a blue ribbon. 'At present, we simply know that the ankh was one of Tutankhamun's most prized possessions. This is clear from your sighting of it on his throne last week. You will need to find your way around Thebes. Edward, I believe you have a working knowledge of the layout of the town based on your recent family holiday to Luxor. I advise you to visit the temples and the palace. I doubt it will be in the tomb that is being built for Tutankhamun. Before I forget, Howard Carter sends his best wishes.'

So that's why Mr Merryweather was dressed as if he'd been to a 1920's golf course.

'You will arrive in Ancient Egypt four years after your last visit. Tutankhamun should be twelve. Watch out for Ay. He will have greater influence at court than the last time you met.'

The Curator waved towards the sarcophagus Johnny was absentmindedly leaning against, and it immediately started to rock backwards and forwards in time to a knocking sound that came from inside. It was the same sound that had scared them a few weeks ago. Johnny leapt away in fright, Ted and Yaz froze, and Mr Merryweather 'harrumphed' as he went to investigate.

The Curator placed his hands on the sarcophagus's painted head and muttered something Johnny couldn't hear until the sarcophagus stopped moving and fell silent.

'Well, well, well,' said Mr Merryweather, tapping the mummy's painted nose. 'It seems that Ay is trying to tell us something from the grave. You will need to be especially vigilant around him. While he claims to be a friend and confidant of Tutankhamun, he is constantly plotting to assume the throne himself. You must also keep an eye on General Horemheb, Tutankhamun's army chief and Ay's rival for the throne. As long as you do not inadvertently alter the course of history, Ay will succeed Tutankhamun. He must still do this, but without the Golden Ankh! So, do you all remember this brief history lesson?'

Johnny shook his head; the complicated Egyptian names had left his mind as soon as they'd entered. Yaz looked as confused as he felt, but he heard Ted say, 'Yes.'

'Edward,' said Mr Merryweather, who looked at them each in turn, 'I will rely on you to remind Jonathon and Yasmin of these few crumbs of historical facts. While you are there, the Time Machine will, of course, be your home, so I have taken the liberty of adding a few more furnishings.'

As soon as they were in the Time Machine, Johnny noticed that the Curator had no idea about appropriate bedding. Each bunk bed had a different coloured pastel duvet cover and pillowcase, patterned with clouds and rainbows, that were suitable for 5 or 6 year-olds. They all stared at them in horror.

'They…' Yaz paused. 'They're lovely.' She walked over to the beds and clambered up to the top bunk. 'I'll have this one.'

'Can I have the bottom one please?' asked Ted.

Johnny wasn't bothered and accepted the middle bunk. 'As long as neither of you snores.'

Mr Merryweather opened the fridge. 'You have provisions for at least five days, just in case.'

They all gazed hungrily into its illuminated interior, packed full of pies, pasties, sausages, yoghurts and milk.

'There is also bread, jam and peanut butter, not to forget sweets, biscuits, chocolate bars and a splendid orange cake. There is plenty of marmalade, of course.'

Johnny felt a shiver of excitement. Two whole days in Ancient Egypt with a sleepover, no parents, and a kitchen full of his favourite food and snacks. The trip was going to be amazing and he was sure they'd do more than just find out where the Golden Ankh was, they'd get their hands on it and bring it back.

15

To the Valley of the Kings

As soon as the Time Machine arrived in Ancient Egypt, Johnny leapt to his feet, determined to look confident. 'Right, let's go.'

Ted slowly uncurled himself out of the ball he'd formed during the journey. 'This is still totally mad, you know?'

Johnny was disappointed to see Yaz had beaten him to action and was already at the wardrobe.

'What are we this time? Street urchins or somebody fancy?' Yaz was holding up a simple rough-looking linen skirt and a fine, white dress. 'What do you think, Queen Yasmin today?'

'I don't think we want to attract attention or anything,' said Ted, now also searching through the clothes. 'Here's what we wore last time.'

Yaz sighed, holding onto the fine, long dress.

'What about somewhere in the, you know, middle?' Johnny agreed with Ted. Looking aristocratic was bound to attract questions they wouldn't be able to answer. However, looking too poor might lead to a whole set of other problems. The street urchin clothes they wore last time had ended up with them almost becoming slaves. Johnny pulled out three sets of clothes that didn't seem too posh or too threadbare. 'Nicely middle of the road, plain and forgettable.'

Within minutes they were changed and standing by the door to the outside. Johnny opened the door and they all looked out as the sun rose over Thebes.

'Where shall we go Ted?' Johnny stepped out into the same sandy street they had been to last week. It was four years since their last visit, but everything looked pretty much the same.

Ted thought for a while. 'Let's go back to the Nile and see if we can get into the temple for a proper look around.'

'Great,' said Yaz, who was clearly keen to get going.

'What about guards?' Johnny didn't want to walk into a trap.

'Shouldn't be as many as at the palace,' Ted replied, 'but maybe we should have a drink first. There's hot chocolate, you know.' Ted looked back longingly at the kitchen.

'We need to get cracking,' replied Johnny. Ted groaned, but Yaz was immediately stuffing chocolate, energy bars, a torch and a water bottle into a cloth bag, which she hid under her tunic.

They were soon on the Avenue of Sphinxes outside Luxor Temple and next to the Nile once again. There were a lot more people on the riverbank than the last time they were here, and Johnny hoped they could just mingle with worshippers going into the temple. He tried to see what was happening and spotted a procession of well-dressed people boarding boats on either side of a large golden barge. A boy was being carried on board the barge and placed on a curtained throne.

'Look, it's Tutankhamun,' said Johnny.

'He's older.' Yaz was peering through the crowd. 'Just like the Curator said.'

'Awesome.' Ted sounded impressed. 'The whole royal court must be here. There's Ay beside Tutankhamun and I bet that thug's General Horemheb.' Ted pointed to a tall muscular man with a scar on his left cheek who stood stiffly on the other side of the throne.

'Let's find a way to get across.' Johnny plunged into the crowd, Yaz following closely behind and Ted catching up.

'That's not our plan,' called Ted.

Johnny ignored him. He hoped they could sneak onto one for a free ride over the Nile. Something drew him towards Tutankhamun's golden barge. It was crazy, but he wanted somehow to save Tutankhamun from Ay. Johnny tried to shake the thought from his mind. There was no way he could change this much history, it wasn't like taking the place of someone in a photo.

As soon as he was beside the golden barge, Johnny decided to go for it. He followed some slaves carrying food and drink and was soon on board. He realised Yaz was pulling a more reluctant Ted onto the barge beside her.

'Made it, despite worry pants,' whispered Yaz. 'Now what?'

Johnny hadn't thought this far ahead. 'Just enjoy the ride?'

'Johnny, we're bound to be caught,' said Ted nervously. 'What about the temple?'

'We'll have a look on our way back.' Johnny was too thrilled to be on Tutankhamun's royal barge to get off again now.

Oarsmen pushed the barge away from the riverbank and started to row towards the other side. It was clear that they would not be on the barge for long. Johnny glanced back and saw three young slaves standing dejected on the riverbank they'd just left.

'Come on you lot, no time to lose.' A large slave thrust three plates into their hands. 'Serve the Pharaoh his treats. Figs, pomegranates and dates.

Kneel in front of him, keep your heads bowed and eyes down.'

'Here we go again,' whispered Johnny as he led Yaz and Ted to the front of the throne. They knelt in a row and each held a plate up to Tutankhamun. Johnny was shaking with nerves as he wondered what would happen if the Pharaoh recognised them from four years ago.

'Do not be afraid, you can look upon me.' Tutankhamun spoke to them gently.

Johnny heard Ay say 'tsk' but he looked up as Tutankhamun took a fig and began to slowly chew it while staring back down at him.

'Do I know you?' Tutankhamun leaned forward. 'You look familiar.'

Johnny shook his head and looked down again. He heard Ted groan.

'Do you think they look familiar Ay?'

'I hardly think so lord.' The Grand Vizier sounded bored. 'I can have them thrown overboard if you wish.'

Tutankhamun laughed. 'We would have no subjects left if we killed everyone you wanted to. I am sure we have met them before. Girl, give me a pomegranate.'

Yaz offered up her plate to Tutankhamun, her head bowed to keep him from seeing her face.

'I order you to look at me,' said Tutankhamun.

Yaz slowly lifted her head.

'That is it,' exclaimed Tutankhamun, looking intently at all three of them. 'You are the street children chosen to become my slaves during my first Festival of Thoth. Ay, see here, they are the children who went missing.'

The Grand Vizier narrowed his eyes. 'They can't be, my lord.'

'I am sure Ay, do not dispute me.' Tutankhamun sounded annoyed. He focused on Johnny. 'You, tell me I am right.'

Johnny didn't know what to say but found himself muttering, 'Yes lord, we are.' Johnny closed his eyes. Was it the right answer?

Tutankhamun clapped his hands in joy. 'Horus be praised for sending you back to me. I told you so, Ay.'

Tutankhamun leant towards them. 'I do believe you haven't aged in four years. It must be a miracle of Horus. You are sent by divine providence.'

The Grand Vizier stared at them suspiciously and fidgeted with a knife in his belt, but they reached the other side of the Nile and everyone started moving. Johnny, Ted and Yaz bowed to Tutankhamun and slipped off the barge with the first servants. They were soon walking with a procession of huge men carrying curtained sedan chairs on their shoulders and passed through groves of date palms, wheat fields, farmhouses and temples towards a gap in the rocky hills ahead. They slotted in between the guards beside Tutankhamun's sedan.

'Slave.' Tutankhamun opened the curtains of the chair and called to Johnny. 'We are visiting my tomb for a ceremony to leave some token of my godliness inside it. This is a very auspicious day for your return.'

Johnny nodded, then gathered his nerves to ask, 'Is it the Golden Ankh?' He prayed Tutankhamun wouldn't be suspicious that he was asking.

'What a curious question,' replied Tutankhamun. 'We are leaving a small statue of Horus. The ankh will only be placed in my tomb after my death.' The Pharaoh patted something out of sight behind his chair. 'Why do you ask?'

'Oh, no reason,' said Johnny.

Tutankhamun glared at him then let the curtains fall closed again.

'Idiot,' whispered Yaz. 'You'll give us away.'

'Someone think of a plan then,' Johnny replied. 'I think he has the ankh with him.'

The procession wound its way along a sandy valley, which Johnny recognised from their visit to see Howard Carter. They hadn't gone far into the valley when they stopped below a building site full of ropes, pulleys and wicker baskets. Piles of broken rock spilled down from a rectangular black gash in the hillside. A ramp of stones led up to the hole.

'This isn't as far into the valley as the tomb we saw in 1922,' said Ted quietly. 'That proves Ay swapped tombs when Tutankhamun died.'

'Help me walk.' Tutankhamun called to Yaz as the pole bearers gently lowered the chair to the ground. The Pharaoh held out his hand.

Yaz hurried forward, took hold of Tutankhamun's hand and steadied him as he stepped down from the sedan chair. He leant on a stick and held on to Yaz as he limped up a rubble path to the tomb entrance.

Johnny let the procession flow around him, hoping to stay by Tutankhamun's sedan and work out a way to get the Golden Ankh, but someone pushed him from behind.

'Get a move on.' It was the Grand Vizier, who was staring menacingly at him. Johnny followed Yaz up the ramp. 'You are the street children from the first year of Tutankhamun's reign! What dark magic is this? How come you look no older?'

Johnny looked away. 'We don't eat much food, sir.'

'There's plenty of fat on you.' Ay pinched Johnny's arm. 'What is a Greek boy doing in Thebes?'

Johnny tried to think of anything he had learnt

about the Ancient Greeks. There was a giant wooden horse at the Battle of Troy and Jason and the Argonauts looked for a golden sheep. Or was the sheep at Troy and the Argonauts sailed in the horse? Did someone kill the Minotaur in the maze with a ball of string? Had any of this happened yet? Ted would know.

'Did we capture your ship?' asked Ay.

'Yes,' muttered Johnny, relieved that Ay answered his own question. 'That's it.'

'I am disappointed, Ay,' said Tutankhamun. 'They have not painted any gods on the walls yet.'

'Thank you, Tutankhamun,' said Johnny to himself. Saved by the Pharaoh.

Ay turned to Tutankhamun and bowed fawningly. 'The work has been delayed by the plague, lord. We have lost many slaves.'

'You did not tell me there was plague in the Valley, Ay. What are you thinking of, bringing me here?' Tutankhamun sounded alarmed. 'Let us conduct the ceremony with the Horus statue as quickly as we can.'

'Yes my lord,' replied Ay.

Johnny, Yaz and Ted watched a shaven-headed priest put the statue inside the tomb door while Tutankhamun stood back holding a cloth over his mouth. The priest sang a few words while he sprinkled water over the statue.

'Let us depart,' said Tutankhamun.

'May I show the three children inside your magnificent tomb?' asked Ay.

'Why would you want to do that, Ay?' Tutankhamun sounded like a bad-tempered teenager.

'Just an indulgence sir, to celebrate their return.'

'If you must. Make sure they do not catch the plague. I do not want to lose them again.' Tutankhamun limped down the ramp. 'Meet me at the barge when you have finished.'

Soon they were left alone with Ay and four guards. Johnny didn't feel good about this.

'I do not know who you are, but I do not trust you.' Ay towered over them. 'Guards, they are Assyrian spies sent to assassinate our Pharaoh. Throw them inside and shut the door. I'll order the work stopped until the plague goes away. When the tomb builders return, tell them to feed the bodies to the vultures.'

Johnny, Ted and Yaz were thrust into the dark tomb and plunged into total blackness as the guards slammed and bolted the wooden door shut behind them. They could hear Ay laughing as he walked away.

16

Lost in Tutankhamun's Tomb

'Right,' said Yaz slowly, 'that didn't go quite how we expected. Good thing I brought my torch.'

She rummaged in her bag and flicked on her torch. It created a small pool of white light on the tomb's floor. She swung it around onto the walls, which were plain, grey and, by the smell of damp limestone that filled the tomb, recently plastered. Johnny tried tugging and pushing the door, but it was firmly shut.

'Have some chocolate,' said Yaz. 'Mum says it's good for shock.'

Johnny and Ted happily munched on a couple of bars. A flickering light caught Johnny's eye in the distance as he peered into the gloom of the long, straight corridor that ran gradually down into the hillside. 'Looks like fire. More guards?'

'I don't think so,' said Ted cautiously. 'I think it's an oil lamp or torch on the wall.'

'Reckon it's a way out?' asked Yaz.

'I have no idea,' replied Ted as he carefully folded the foil from his chocolate and stuffed it in Yaz's bag. 'Better not freak out the future Egyptologists.'

'I thought you knew everything,' snorted Yaz. She passed around the water bottle. 'Just a sip, we better keep most of it for later.'

This was getting a bit too much like Survival mode in Minecraft with no weapons, thought Johnny, and no way of knowing whether they were in Peaceful or Hard. He imagined zombies and creepers hiding in the dark. After a while, he said, 'Let's head straight towards the light and hope there's another entrance. And stick together.'

'I wasn't planning on going anywhere by myself.' Ted's shaky voice made Johnny nervous. He felt he should say something that sounded confident to reassure Ted and Yaz, but he couldn't think of anything, so he just walked determinedly forward. Everything beyond Yaz's torch beam was dark and it all seemed hopeless.

They quickly reached the spluttering, smokey lamp. It was just a bundle of oil-soaked rushes in a small clay pot but it gave out enough light to brighten a patch of the wall behind it and show they were at a crossroads. Rows of similar lamps ran into the distance in all three other directions.

Even in the gloom, they could tell that the tomb builders had barely started the corridors straight ahead and to the left. They hardly went any distance before ending in blank rock with piles of chipped stones, tools and baskets. The corridor to their right kept going until the row of lamps disappeared into the black void.

Johnny counted at least ten lamps before they blurred into each other. This looked more promising, but also worrying, as they couldn't tell what might be living down there.

'This way.' Johnny set off down the corridor. 'If there's another entrance, it must be down here, don't you reckon Ted?'

'There isn't going to be one, I just know it,' replied Ted. 'The tomb's nowhere near finished.'

'Come on, we have to try.' Johnny took a step forward and was met with a gust of cold wind from the far end of the corridor. The temperature suddenly dropped, making them shiver, and Johnny was sure he heard hissing, like escaping gas, but everything became silent again as the wind passed by.

The lamps flickered in the breeze, and the nearest one flared momentarily brighter, lighting up the wall long enough for them to see a painted figure dance and loom out of the wall before it receded into shadows.

'Seth!' Ted yelped and stepped backwards.

Johnny couldn't work out if the figure was human, animal or something in between. He just had time to see what looked like the body and legs of a person, holding a crook and an ankh. But the head was that of a creature with a long snout, like maybe a jackal or an anteater. The figure looked into the tunnel.

'Creepy. Who is Seth?' Even Yaz's voice was shaking, just a little, noticed Johnny.

'God of Chaos and Violence,' said Ted, very quietly. 'He murdered his brother, Osiris.'

'That doesn't sound too good.' Yaz shone her torch along the wall where they saw a second Seth, then another and another. Creepy is right, thought Johnny.

'Seth is always depicted in tombs, it's no big deal.' Ted sounded strangely confident and Johnny realised his friend's knowledge was helping him deal with all of this.

'Let's just check out this tunnel then,' said Yaz. 'If there's no other way out then we'll work out how to break down the door.'

They followed the apparently endless line of Seths deeper into the tomb. Johnny was sure he could hear the hissing sound again, but it was right on the edge of his hearing, too quiet to be sure if it was a real sound rather than ringing in his ears.

'Is it my imagination, or is it getting colder?' Ted's voice trembled, whether with cold or fear Johnny couldn't work out, but he felt Ted was right.

'Is it because we've gone further?' asked Johnny.

'Well.' Ted tried to adopt his know-it-all voice, but he was shaking too much. 'Caves should have a constant temperature and a tomb is just like a cave.'

'And what's that hissing?' Now Yaz's voice wavered.

'You can hear it?' Johnny felt strangely relieved.

'Me too,' whispered Ted. 'It sounds closer now.'

17

Attack of the Snake God

Another wind came howling at them from the far end of the tomb and this time it blew out all but one of the lamps, plunging them into almost total darkness. The faint beam from Yaz's torch was a welcome patch of light, but it didn't carry very far. Johnny caught a whiff of the woody, musky smell again but was more worried by the sound of slithering getting closer and louder. Johnny imagined a giant snake uncoiling in the blackness, then wished he hadn't. Yaz shone her torch in the direction of the sound. Ted screamed, Yaz gulped and Johnny felt his legs go to jelly. Slithering towards them was a massive, dark green and black snake with gleaming, malevolent yellow eyes and a long blood-red tongue that whipped in and out of its mouth, where two scimitar-like fangs dripped green venom.

'Ap-Ap-Apophis,' stammered Ted, frozen in

fear.

The snake fixed its gaze on Ted and flexed its body, scales sliding against each other as it brought its tail over its head until it filled the corridor.

'Come on,' called Johnny, and started to turn away to run.

'No.' Yaz sounded strangely calm and stopped Johnny in his tracks. 'It will be faster than us.'

Ted still hadn't moved and Johnny watched in horror as the snake slipped its tail around him.

'Ted!' Johnny leapt forwards, forgetting his fear to save his friend. He grabbed one of the snake's coils that encircled Ted and tried to pull it away, but it was no good. The snake coiled further and further around and up Ted, tightening all the time. Ted was completely bound, his arms by his sides and eyes bulging in terror.

'Yaz, help me free Ted.' Johnny was shocked to see Yaz rooted to the spot as she gazed up into the snake's eyes. Johnny glanced up at the snake's fangs and had to swallow hard to stop himself from screaming and running away. The snake's eyes were fixed on Yaz, its tongue flicking in and out of its huge mouth as it hissed. Then it roared; a loud, deep, rumbling roar that shook the tomb. Dust and rocks showered them from the roof. Johnny thought two things almost simultaneously. Snakes aren't meant to roar and why doesn't Yaz move? He closed his eyes and waited for the snake to strike. When he realised he was still alive, he looked up. The snake seemed to be taunting him, swaying from side to side as if choosing the best place to bite. Johnny glanced back at Yaz and realised the snake was mirroring the movements she was making with her torch.

Ted made a sound, somewhere between a whimper and a wheeze.

'Hold on!' Johnny sprang back into action and clambered up the snake's coils to get nearer to Ted, whose face was now dark purple. Ted tried to say something, but the snake was too tightly coiled around him, and he was barely breathing.

'Please Ted, what is it?' Johnny desperately pulled at the highest coil.

Ted tried to speak again and managed to slowly force out one word at a time, barely even a whisper, each separated by a long pause. 'Apophis … Snake … God … Fire … Kick … Left … Foot.'

By the time Ted whispered the last word he was so quiet Johnny had his ear right beside Ted's mouth to make out what his friend was saying. Johnny racked his brains to try and work out what the words could mean. They seemed so random. It was obvious this wasn't just a giant snake, it was a monster. Ted must be saying it's a god called Apophis. So how are you supposed to fight a god?

That was when Johnny realised Ted was giving him instructions. He had to do this. Johnny squeezed his hands into tight fists and yelled to encourage himself. As he did so, he felt pins and needles surge through his body and he leapt, further than he thought possible, back to the floor and wrenched the last spluttering, half-dead oil lamp from the wall. The tingling seemed to give him the energy and courage to run back towards the snake, shouting and waving the lamp. The snake reared away and Johnny knew he had something it didn't like. Ted's words must be things the snake hated. Johnny thought as quickly as he could and brandished the lamp towards the snake. It narrowed its eyes and recoiled backwards. Hope rose in Johnny's heart and he lunged at the nearest of the snake's coils, kicking it in anger and fear. Everywhere he struck, the snake's scales blistered and frothed. The snake slithered further away, so Johnny attacked again and chased the snake down the tunnel. He felt triumphant until he realised it was dragging Ted with it. Johnny frantically jumped onto the coils strangling Ted, stamping at them with his left foot. He sensed Yaz beside him, awoken from her trance, kicking at the snake too. A fearsome roar shook down another cascade of dust and plaster from the roof of the tomb. Johnny ducked, but his heart leapt as he felt the coils loosen around Ted, scales blackening and twisting where he had attacked, white foam bubbling up between them. Suddenly, the coils sprang apart, flinging Johnny, Yaz and Ted onto the tunnel floor. The snake slid away, back into the pitch black of the tunnel.

'Ted? Ted, can you hear me?' Johnny shook Ted, who lay still and breathless.

'You keep that snake beast away,' Yaz commanded, pushing Johnny towards Apophis, who was writhing and watching them warily from the darkness.

'Right, let's hope I can remember my first aid.' Yaz pinched Ted's nose between the fingers of one hand, lifted his chin with her other hand so that his head was tilted back, and breathed slowly and repeatedly into his mouth, before pressing down on his chest again and again. Ted stayed motionless and Yaz repeated the whole process until, after what seemed like forever, Ted coughed and his chest heaved in and out as he fought for breath.

Johnny shouted in relief, then heard the snake hissing and sliding towards them again, so he turned and walked towards it, waving the lamp. The snake blenched then slithered further away down the dark tunnel until only its yellow eyes were visible. Johnny resisted the temptation to run after it. Instead, he backed away, keeping his eyes on it, until he was beside Ted and Yaz.

'Come on, let's get out of here before Apotty-whoever the monstrous snake decides we're snack food again,' said Johnny.

'Ted, can you get up?' Yaz asked gently. Johnny could tell she was trying to stay as calm as possible, but her voice was shaking.

Ted nodded. 'I think so.' His voice was barely a whisper, 'It's pronounced Apophis, but it's just a myth.'

'Seemed pretty real to me,' replied Yaz.

Ted tried to stand, but his legs buckled under him and Yaz hauled him to his feet.

'Ouch! My ribs,' screamed Ted. 'They really, really hurt.'

'Can you walk?' Johnny kept his eyes on the snake, which was edging slowly forwards once more. They had to get a move on, somehow, before it decided it was safe to strike again.

'I reckon so.' Ted carefully took a couple of steps while Yaz supported him with one arm and shone her torch ahead of them with her other hand. Johnny followed backwards, so he could vaguely wave the dying oil lamp as threateningly as possible at Apophis. The lamp was, frighteningly, almost out. Apophis followed for a short distance then stopped as if it had hit an invisible barrier it couldn't cross.

'I don't think the monster snake is following us,' said Johnny. He was relieved to see Ted starting to walk more easily after a few steps, though it was still little more than a painful shuffle. 'How are we going to get out?' Johnny knew there was no way they'd get past Apophis to find another entrance.

'We'll have to think of something, won't we?' Yaz replied curtly.

It seemed to take forever to reach the door they had been pushed through. Johnny leant all his weight against it but it was definitely not moving. He felt despair overwhelm him, trapped in a tomb, that was probably full of plague germs, with an evil snake monster for company. Things really weren't going their way.

'What's over there?' Yaz shone her torch into a corner of the wall. There looked to be a hole near the floor. Johnny raced over to it and stuck his hand inside, hoping there were no poisonous spiders or scorpions. The hole was longer than his arm. 'Bring your torch, Yaz.'

They peered into the hole, which continued beyond the reach of the torchlight. Johnny dared hope. 'A tunnel?'

'Could be,' croaked Ted. 'Tomb builders often built secret tunnels so they could come back later and steal the treasure.'

Johnny stared at the hole. It was just large enough for him to crawl into. He didn't think he'd be able to wriggle backwards though. 'Right Yaz, give me your torch and I'll try it. If there's a way out, I'll shout. If not, I guess I'm stuck.'

Without thinking about it further, Johnny lay down and slowly inched his way into the narrow tunnel, his arms stretched out in front of him. Rough stones grazed his skin and he could hardly breathe. He'd just decided this was madness and he'd be stuck in the hill forever when the torch shone on a pile of stones that blocked his way. This is the end, thought Johnny despondently as he tried to push at the rocks. To his surprise, they moved and, after working his hands in between the stones, they all fell away in a clatter that sounded like they were tumbling down the hillside. Warm, sweet air rushed over him and he reached forward again and felt — nothing. With an effort that cost him, even more, scratches and grazes, he wormed his way out onto the steep hillside. He nearly slipped as he bent down and called into the tunnel. 'I'm out. Come NOW!'

Eventually, Ted then Yaz crawled out of the tunnel. They dusted themselves down and looked around. They were halfway up the hillside and could see the ramp they had walked up earlier. The sun was setting and, in the last glimmer of daylight, they made their way down to the valley and back to the Nile, holding up Ted the whole way, who kept moaning about his ribs hurting. It was almost dark by the time they reached the river and no boats were going between the two sides. Johnny groaned to himself. How were they going to get across?

'Here.' Yaz thrust the end of a rope into his hands. 'Grab this.'

She was kneeling in a small boat made from bundles of reeds that was hidden against the riverbank. It had been tied to a post and Yaz had an arm around the post to stop the boat from floating away on the current.

'Wake up, Johnny,' she hissed. 'Get the rope.'

Johnny grabbed the rope and quickly pulled it towards him while Yaz fed it through her free hand.

'I'm not sure we should steal a boat,' whispered Ted.

'How else do you plan to get across the river?' Yaz replied. 'Just keep hold of that rope. Ted, you get in first,' she ordered.

Ted cautiously placed one foot in the boat, which dipped alarmingly under his weight. He was about to lift his foot straight back out, but Yaz grabbed hold of his arm and pulled him flat on his face onto the bottom of the boat. It rocked so much they were soon soaked with river water.

'Whaaaar,' yelled Ted.

'Shhhh,' said Johnny.

'Shut up and stay still Ted,' whispered Yaz. 'Johnny, you push us off.'

Johnny leant down and pushed against the

bundles of rushes that curved upwards to create the end of the boat. With a sucking noise, it bobbed away from the muddy riverbank and started to float with the current. Johnny almost toppled into the river as he held on to the boat while his feet remained stuck in the mud. With a heave, he pulled his feet free and managed to half-leap, half-fall into the boat, where he sat down with a thump. They were floating out of control as the boat began to spin around. Ted gripped the sides of the boat tightly and looked like he was about to be sick any second, but Yaz picked up a paddle and slid it into the water. She turned the boat to face the opposite riverbank and was soon powering them across.

'Canoe weekends,' said Yaz.

18

Most Afflictions Cured 98.3% of the Time

They eventually reached the Time Machine with Ted, who could barely walk and was almost passing out by the time they were safely back inside. Ted slumped into one of the chairs with a moan and clutched his sides.

'What are we going to do, Yaz?' Johnny could see scarily big dark purple bruises forming on Ted's arms and legs.

'Let's see what Mr Merryweather's first aid kit has in it that's good for being crushed by a giant, evil, snake that shouldn't exist and no one told us about,' said Yaz angrily as she stomped off to the find the large, green box. 'Or whether it cures the plague.' She imitated the Curator, 'I can reassure you that by visiting the time of Pharaoh Tutankhamun you will not die of a curse.'

Johnny sat down with Ted. Yaz had been complaining about the Curator for not warning them about the snake monster the whole way back from the tomb. She had almost convinced Johnny that he was a dangerous old fool, just as his mum had told them, and they should not come back to the museum once they were home. Johnny had expected an adventure, but he'd thought it would be a game of dodging guards and soldiers, not fighting monsters. He wondered what else the Curator hadn't told them about — man-eating Griffins, gods with the heads of dogs, giant crocodiles? They might have the plague as well and he didn't have a clue how to tell! Mr Merryweather gave the impression of knowing pretty much everything, so why hadn't he told them that magical beasts might actually be alive? Johnny felt angry at the Curator for hiding stuff from them that could kill them. The idea of running around Ancient Egypt didn't feel that much of an adventure any more.

Yaz dragged the first aid box over to Ted. Close up, it was made from some sort of incredibly smooth, dark green metal that seemed to absorb light, the sort of thing that featured in TV programmes about alien technology and the US airforce. There was a large, white cross and the words New Haven Hospital on the lid. Below this was written First and Emergency Aid for all Types of Atomic and Molecular Injuries, Accidents and Near-Death Experiences. Most Common and Unusual Afflictions Cured 98.3% of the Time. This was very different from the small, green plastic first aid kit his mum kept behind the toaster. Johnny passed his hand across the letters but snatched it away when he felt the box hum and tingle ever so slightly.

'What do you think's inside?' asked Ted cautiously. He winced in pain with every word and his bruises were looking uglier with each second that passed.

Yaz clicked open the fasteners and lifted the lid. As they looked inside, their faces were lit by a cool, green glow, which immediately calmed Johnny's nerves. Rather than the usual few plasters, tangle of bandages, scissors and plastic gloves that he was expecting to see, the box was packed full of old-fashioned bottles with glass stoppers that surrounded a flat disc of milky coloured glass set in a brass frame. At one end of the frame was a dial with a red arrow that you could turn to point at the names of illnesses and injuries, which arranged in rings around the dial. The types of injuries became more extreme the further away they were from the dial. The closest ring included headache, toothache, cuts, bruising, being sick and bee sting, while the outermost ones were heavy bleeding, blindness, deafness, loss of a limb and being crushed.

As he reached towards the dial, the box spoke with a soothing electronic voice spoke from inside the box, while the words appeared on the inside of the lid like hazy subtitles.

'Welcome to First and Emergency Aid for all Types of Atomic and Molecular Injuries, Accidents and Near-Death Experiences.'

'Need Medical Assistance?'

'Are you feeling a bit poorly?'

'Have you had an accident or emergency, or both?'

They all looked at each other.

'Come on, don't be shy, have you been crushed by a giant, mythical creature you had no idea existed?'

The words of this last question hovered inside the lid a little longer.

'Yes,' answered Johnny uncertainly.

The box spoke again, this time each word appeared in turn to fill the inside of the lid. 'Then Do Not Waste Time! Put your hand on the diagnostic touchscreen.' There was a slight pause as the word 'touchscreen' lingered inside the box lid accompanied by sparkles of cascading light.

'What's that, fairy dust?' snorted Yaz.

'Do it now,' said the voice more firmly, the

words shining a little brighter than before. 'Slow Reactions May Lead to DEATH!!!'

'OK, OK,' shouted Johnny, annoyed by the First Aid Kit's tone. 'Ted, quick, just do what this thing says.'

Ted leant forward and put his right hand on the milky glass touchscreen. Johnny turned the dial to BEING CRUSHED' and the touchscreen lit up a pale green while the box hummed.

'It tickles,' muttered Ted, his frown quickly disappearing. 'Ooh, it's ever so soothing.'

The box spoke at them again. 'Patient 4-0-0-9, what have you been doing to yourself? You are in a right state.' There was a pause, and Johnny was sure the First Aid Kit was thinking. 'Diagnosis is now complete. Please stand up and face the First and Emergency Aid for all Types of Atomic and Molecular Injuries, Accidents and Near-Death Experiences. All other parties, do stand back.'

Johnny and Yaz moved away and Ted slowly tried to stand up while keeping his hand on the touchscreen.

'I mean straight up.'

Ted snatched his hand off the touchscreen and stood upright.

'Good. Now please try to stand still,' commanded the voice, 'to ensure treatment is successful.'

A delicate set of ornate, brass panels unfurled from inside the box on thin rods, accompanied by a variety of whirrs, clicks and beeps. Eventually, it formed a screen around Ted and he stepped back slightly as it glowed to bathe him in more of the soothing, cooling, green light.

'I can feel the pain going away,' said Ted in surprise.

'Wow, look at your bruises,' exclaimed Johnny.

Ted looked all over his arms and down at his legs. The bruises were rapidly vanishing as his skin returned to its normal colour.

The light flicked off and the panels retracted back into the box.

'Molecular restoration of skin and muscle tissue is complete,' crooned the voice. 'Please take the medicine indicated, following the instructions on the label. Have a relatively pain-free day.'

The bottles were rotating around the touchscreen, clanking against each other, until they stopped and one bottle rose above the others, spinning slowly. It was filled with a glowing white liquid. Ted nervously picked it out of the First Aid Kit and read the label out loud.

'For healing broken ribs and crushed muscles. Take two teaspoons right this instant, put me back and have a nice lie-down.' A teaspoon popped up.

Ted looked worried. 'This is all a bit weird. It's

not like our local hospital.'

'Just get on and drink it,' said Yaz.

Ted winced with pain as he took the spoon and poured the first measure. It glowed and had a sweet, metallic smell mixed with mints. Ted closed his eyes, swallowed the spoonful in one gulp and pulled a face.

Yaz grinned. 'Go on then, second spoonful.' She was enjoying Ted's discomfort but did produce some sweets. 'These will take the taste away,' she said.

Ted gulped down the second spoonful, then stuffed a handful of sweets into his mouth while trying to say 'yuk' and went to lie down on the bunk beds. After a few seconds of chewing and swallowing sweets, he said, 'I hope I'll be OK.'

Johnny anxiously watched Ted squirm and wriggle as if there was an itch he couldn't scratch. Eventually, Ted lay still, eyes closed, beads of sweat on his forehead.

'Ted,' Johnny asked nervously, 'Ted, are you OK?'

Suddenly, Ted sat upright, smiling. 'I don't think I've ever felt better.'

They all high-fived each other. The First Aid Kit interrupted them with a polite cough.

'Not so fast, I have detected something else. Please all come over here.'

They didn't dare disobey the First Aid Kit, so stood in front of it as three small vials of purple liquid rose above the other jars.

'Who has been silly enough to contract Bubonic Plague? No hand-washing or face masks I assume.'

They all looked at each other in shock.

'The plague? Isn't that, like, deadly?' asked Yaz.

'Wiped out most of Europe in the Middle Ages,' replied Ted, looking glum.

'Now, now, no need to fear. First and Emergency Aid for all Types of Atomic and Molecular Injuries, Accidents and Near-Death Experiences is here! Oh, I quite like that. Simply drink a full bottle of medicine each, and you will be right as rain in no time.'

The medicine tasted disgusting and they all stuffed as many sweets as they could into their mouths straight after. Ted pressed the red HOME button and they all collapsed into the red chairs as the Time Machine began to rattle, hum and shake. Johnny closed his eyes and tried to relax, but he felt let down by Mr Merryweather, while Ted and Yaz complained about the Curator for the short journey back to their own time.

19

Anger Before Christmas

'What do you think you're playing at?' Yaz stormed over to Mr Merryweather as soon as he entered the Time Machine on their return. The Curator stepped backwards, throwing his hands up to protect himself as if Yaz was going to attack. 'We could have been killed back there. We were locked in a tomb, Ted was crushed by a giant monstrous snake and we caught the plague. You knew there'd be something like that, didn't you? Didn't you? What next, gods of death, the devil?'

Silence hung heavily between them. Johnny went over to the table to spread marmalade on the first batch of toast that pinged out of the toaster. The aches of time travel were quickly replaced by the warm, comforting sensation that Johnny had come to expect from eating the marmalade. Ted sat on a chair next to him, but Johnny was too restless to sit down. Yaz screamed in frustration at Mr

Merryweather's silence and eventually accepted the slice of toast and marmalade Johnny handed her.

Mr Merryweather eventually sighed. 'Please tell me more.'

Johnny got as far as saying how they had sneaked onto the royal barge and that Tutankhamun recognised them when Yaz interrupted.

'We nearly got killed three times because of you,' Yaz said angrily. She told Mr Merryweather about being trapped in the tomb by Ay, their fight with the snake and Ted being crushed. 'And then we found out we all had the plague!' she shouted.

Mr Merryweather listened in silence.

'Why don't you say anything?' Yaz waved a second piece of toast around so violently that a dollop of marmalade flew off and landed on Mr Merryweather's jacket.

'I hadn't realised the Shadow Lord was now able to do that,' said Mr Merryweather, picking off the marmalade and sticking it in his mouth.

'Do what?' demanded Yaz.

'I must sincerely apologise. Yes, I have kept some information from you.'

'I told you,' said Yaz turning to Johnny and Ted.

Johnny felt deflated. He had trusted the Curator.

'However, let me explain. Would you please sit down Yasmin and Jonathon, it will help tidy the place up a little.'

Johnny stared at Mr Merryweather; he didn't feel like sitting down.

'As you wish,' continued Mr Merryweather. 'I had not expected you to encounter one of the elemental beings, mythical creatures if you like.'

Yaz sighed and crossed her arms, scowling at the Curator.

'You see, the beasts and monsters, gods and goddesses, of legends all exist.'

Ted nearly choked on his piece of toast. 'Impossible.'

The Curator held up his hand. 'I know it can be difficult for those brought up in the rational, modern, world to believe this. I have tried before to educate others. No one has believed me because, until now, no one has encountered such a creature. Elemental beings are brought into existence by the sheer willpower of belief. If enough people believe in them strongly enough they can appear, but only at times when they are summoned or during times of great joy or fear.'

By now, Johnny realised they were all sitting down, staring at Mr Merryweather. Yaz still shot the Curator angry glances and Ted just shook his head.

'Edward, once again it is about the quantum nature of the universe. Ironically, the more scientifically advanced we have become, the less understanding of quantum matter we have. You are aware of the theory of quantum entanglement, are you not Edward?'

Johnny didn't have a clue what the Curator was talking about, however, Ted nodded.

'A sub-atomic particle in one part of the universe can directly affect another particle, even if they are light years apart,' said Ted.

'Indeed.' Mr Merryweather cleared his throat. 'I have said that we can manipulate particles with our minds if we learn how to. I know you are sceptical Edward but I guess that Johnny and Yaz may have done this to rescue you without knowing.'

'I did feel pins and needles again,' said Johnny, 'but there wasn't anything magical.'

'You do not call saving Edward from Apophis magical?' asked Mr Merryweather. 'I do, magical and incredibly brave of you and Yaz. You have read, no doubt, of a mother lifting a car off a trapped child and telling the press that she did not know how she found the strength to do so? That is the same.

'Large groups of people can also influence particles through their beliefs or strong emotions such as fear, anger and love. Let us take dragons, for example. They existed in medieval Europe and ancient China, brought into existence by the sheer, unshakeable belief of thousands of people. They did not appear all the time but were made real at times such as battles, earthquakes or terrible storms. This is why we never find their bones.'

'Rubbish,' exclaimed Ted.

'Difficult to believe, I know. The Ancient Egyptians had an absolute belief in their gods, and the gods took real form from time to time. Egyptian priests channelled this belief in their temples to such an extent that the magical would happen.'

This was way too much for Johnny. Gods, monsters and magic could exist after all? Ted was still shaking his head and muttering under his breath.

'I see you do not believe me. Yet, how do you explain Apophis appearing in the tomb? Congratulations on recognising him by the way, that saved your life, with the help of your friends' quick actions of course.' Mr Merryweather indicated Johnny and Yaz with a sweep of his arm. 'You are quite the team.'

There was silence, eventually broken by Johnny. 'Don't forget the Sphinx last time.'

'The Sphinx?' Mr Merryweather arched an eyebrow. 'Explain please Jonathon.'

'We didn't have time to tell you, we had to solve a riddle set by a Sphinx. Ted got it right.'

'Is this correct?' asked Mr Merryweather.

Ted nodded.

Mr Merryweather put his thumbs behind his

lapels and began pacing the Time Machine. 'A Sphinx I can imagine. They are ten a penny in some places. The real worry is Apophis and how it appeared in the tomb. The three of you clearly could not have thought it into existence, while the lack of any Egyptians in the tomb rules out local fears. It would take a huge crowd and strong emotions to do that. I fear that the Shadow Lord manifested Apophis. He must somehow have access to an Ancient Egyptian or a historian of Egypt. On the bright side, I see you have successfully used the First Aid Kit. You now know how well it can protect and heal you from almost any injury or illness. You only need to make sure you reach it in time.'

Johnny was too tired to say anything. Yaz and Ted were still scowling.

Mr Merryweather continued, 'Please let me remind you, the ability to travel through time is a rare and special talent. There are very few of you in the world and to find three time travellers in one small town is almost miraculous. However, being able to time travel is one thing, knowing how to deal with dangerous situations in the strange world of the past is rarer still.'

Johnny had never felt special or important before, and this was far better than being good at maths or football. Different emotions competed for attention, joy and pride mixed with anger and fear.

Mostly, he just wanted to go home.

The Curator left them and soon they were showered, dressed for school and eating lunch with their schoolmates in the Buxton Hall. The marmalade-making machine was still producing jar after jar as it vented steam from various valves. Johnny glanced at his friends; it didn't look like they'd just been to Ancient Egypt and fought Apophis. Even more crazy was how it was just lunchtime. They quietly took their lunch boxes, found an empty table and munched on their sandwiches and wraps in silence. The others occasionally glanced over in their direction, but they clearly didn't see anything suspicious and he was a bit disappointed he didn't look like the conqueror of a fearsome monster. He had a desire for everyone else to cheer him. After lunch, they all helped move some boxes from one room to another. Ted and Yaz whispered that they were not going back to Egypt again, it was too dangerous and Mr Merryweather could not be trusted.

Alisha and Emily came over to Johnny.

'What have you all been up to then?' asked Emily.

'You look like you've seen a ghost,' said Alisha.

'And you've got sand in your hair,' said Emily with a grin.

Johnny didn't have the energy to come up with

a story so he just smiled back.

Before they left, Mr Merryweather quietly said, 'I do hope you all return next week.'

* * *

The next few weeks dragged painfully by, despite Christmas fast approaching. Johnny couldn't concentrate on anything and kept getting into trouble with his teachers, including five detentions with Mr Leadbitter. Jordan managed to find him at least once a day with no teachers around to taunt him in front of his rugby friends. Ted missed the rest of Museum Club before the end of term. He was ill the same day each week, conveniently, thought Johnny, who was sure Ted was avoiding the museum. Mr Merryweather didn't let them return to Egypt. He said that all three of them had to travel together and that he needed to rethink their strategy in light of the encounter with Apophis. Johnny was desperate to go back to Thebes, but whenever he tried talking about it, Ted changed the subject and Yaz said she wanted more time to make up her mind. Johnny felt in limbo. On one walk to school, he told Ted and Yaz he'd found the last trip to Egypt exciting, even battling Apophis, and that defeating the snake showed they were good. Ted flew into a rage, shouting about how he had nearly been killed, and stormed off ahead of them.

'That wasn't a good idea Johnny,' said Yaz.

'But, I'm fed up. Do you know what our mission means to me Yaz?'

'No, tell me.' Yaz put her hands on her hips as if challenging him.

'Escape, that's what. Escape from this boring town, from Mr Leadbitter and Jordan.' Johnny stopped. 'Oh never mind, you've never been bullied.'

'No? How do you know?'

'You're always telling mum how many friends you have, how popular you are.'

'Maybe that's because I think that's what she wants to hear, Johnny.'

'What about your cricket team, the other runners, people at your jujitsu club?'

'Just other kids I play sport with.'

'But…'

'But nothing.' Yaz snapped at him. 'It isn't easy being one of the few Asian kids at school, you know. Sport lets me be respected for what I can do, for a brief while, but it always ends as soon as we stop.'

'Sorry Yaz, I didn't know. You're…' Johnny looked away.

'Yes?'

'Well, you're like a sister and that's probably why I keep fighting with you. I'd miss you.'

Yaz wiped a tear away. 'That's the nicest thing

you've ever said to me.'

Johnny shrugged. 'I didn't realise it until we fought Apophis. We've lived next door to each other ever since I can remember, and you've always liked different things to me. I'm sorry for shouting.'

'Never mind.' Yaz glanced at her watch. 'Look, we'll be late unless we get a move on. And Johnny…'

'Yes?'

'Thank you.'

20

A Tight Spot While Christmas Shopping

For Johnny, the start of the Christmas holiday brought relief from school but it was pretty boring because Ted and Yaz weren't around and his mum worked hard to finish for Christmas. Ted's family went on a pre-Christmas visit to his mum's relatives in London. Thankfully, this wasn't a year when they stayed the whole holiday with his dad's family in Barbados, so Ted would be at home on Christmas Day. Yaz was packed off to stay with her grandparents while her mum and dad spent long hours at the warehouse during their busiest time of the year. Johnny had never missed Yaz before but realised how much they had become friends as a result of her breaking into Museum Club. His anger about that was now a distant memory. This year, Yaz was even going to join Johnny and Ted on

Christmas Day to check out each other's presents.

He went into the town centre one cold, windy day to buy presents for his mum and aunts, Ted and Yaz. He enjoyed choosing things he knew Ted would like but had previously just put up with buying something for Yaz under his mum's orders. Yaz's family didn't celebrate Christmas but had the holiday off work and loads of family around. Her parents always told his mum that she shouldn't buy presents for them but every year she did. Johnny was determined to buy her something nice, which he had thought about, rather than just grabbing the first pink thing he saw. He wanted to say thank you for how cool she'd been in Egypt but he also hoped to change her mind about not going back to Thebes.

It was almost dark and starting to sleet when Johnny left the last shop, happy with what he had bought. The town was busy with people rushing to fit their shopping in before Christmas Day and the pavement was packed. Someone was shouting 'hot chestnuts,' a brass band was belting out carols and the Christmas lights sparkled above the street. Johnny felt the happiest he had all holiday but his good mood was shattered as he walked into a large, immovable object blocking the pavement. It was Jordan.

Jordan pushed Johnny and sent him sprawling, presents and bags scattering everywhere.

'Oh dear,' smirked Jordan, who took two steps forward, bent down and hauled Johnny to his feet by his scarf. Johnny saw one bag kicked into the road by a shopper too busy to spot it in time.

'Little Johnny's presents for his mummy are in the gutter, what a shame.' Jordan gave Johnny's scarf a twist.

Johnny realised he was scared, though he tried to tell himself to stop being silly. He'd fought a monstrous, mythical snake in Tutankhamun's tomb, surely he could deal with Jordan these days. The thought was squeezed out of his mind as Jordan tightened his scarf once more and pulled him so close he was nose-to-nose with Jordan's angry, contorted face. Johnny was sure somebody would notice, but everyone was shrouded in hats and scarves against the wind and sleet as they rushed by to get their Christmas shopping done on time. Johnny wished Yaz and Ted were here, they were a team, they were stronger together. He twisted his face away from Jordan's and saw, from the corner of his eye, a woman stopping by his bag in the gutter and stooping down to pick it up. He could just make out the hem of a long, thick coat, a brown dress and old-fashioned shoes.

'Excuse me,' said the stranger, 'I suggest you let go.'

Jordan growled, almost like a dog, and the

stranger's feet approached closer.

'I say, did you hear me?' insisted the stranger.

'None of your business, shove off,' snarled Jordan.

'Oh, but I am rather afraid that it is my business,' replied the stranger, coming closer still.

Through water-filled eyes, Johnny saw the stranger take something small and brass from inside her coat, flick a small switch and the object glowed orange. Instantly, Jordan let go of Johnny's scarf and slumped to the pavement. He looked unconscious.

'Are you hurt?' The stranger had a kindly voice that reassured Johnny. She took Johnny by the elbow and walked him away. 'There is no need to worry, I have your shopping bags.'

Johnny's neck hurt, his heart was thumping and he felt light-headed. 'Erm, thanks, right.' It was as if someone else was speaking.

'Are you truly all right?' The stranger looked intently at him, her eyes glinting from the shadow of a wide-brimmed hat.

Johnny closed his eyes for a second to bring himself back to earth. He rubbed his neck, where a red mark was blossoming. 'I think so, thank you Mrs…'

'Please,' the woman held up a hand, 'do not mention it. It is always good to help a fellow traveller, especially someone thoughtful enough to buy Christmas presents for his companions. They will be delighted. I am sure all will be well.'

With that, the stranger handed Johnny his bags and, with a slight nod of her head, walked away. She must know about their quest thought Johnny. He had the impression that he should know her but she was soon lost among the crowd. Johnny looked down at Jordan, heard someone mutter 'scruffy hooligan' and went home.

21

The Shadow Lord for Christmas

Johnny screamed and kicked at the snake as he wrestled with it in the pitch black until it stopped moving and collapsed to the soft ground like a lifeless husk. He breathed slowly in and realised he was screwing his eyes tight shut, so he blinked them open to see the illuminated red outline of a number 7 flip over to 8. The ragged foe lay motionless in his hands and he sighed. He had defeated his duvet. Again. It was just another dream about fighting Apophis. As the snake faded away and he relished the warm comfort of his duvet, he remembered it was Christmas Day. He leapt out of bed, burst into his mum's still-dark room and woke her up too.

'Merry Christmas Mum!' he shouted.

She fumbled for her bedside light and smiled back at him. 'Merry Christmas Jonathon!'

'Race you downstairs.'

'That's not fair.' His mum pretended to sound

annoyed. 'You have a head start!'

Soon they were both opening presents, Johnny frantically tearing the paper off one parcel after another, despite his mum telling him to slow down and 'appreciate what people have given you'. Didn't she know by now that there was no chance he'd open presents slowly? His mum still hadn't opened most of her presents when he'd finished his, so he helped her until she insisted they have breakfast and take a good look at what he'd been given. As usual, she'd been quietly keeping a list of who had sent them what so they could write thank you cards, which included his two aunts, an uncle he hardly ever saw, some cousins he'd barely met and Ted. His mum was pleased with the presents he'd bought her, despite the fact he didn't have much money to spend.

All too soon, it was the worst part of Christmas Day — dinner — which always involved too much food he didn't like and took up too long in the middle of the day when he'd rather be playing with his new games. Worst of all, his aunts came for dinner every year, which meant he'd have to dress smartly and be on his best behaviour while they asked him endless questions about how he was doing at school. Then they'd talk about boring stuff with his mum, mostly about which relative he'd never heard of had died that year, before making veiled comments about his dad that he wasn't meant to understand but which made it clear they had never approved of him right from the start. Then, after dinner, they'd drink sherry, complain that no one made Babycham anymore, and watch a boring old musical on TV. But, once he'd cleared the table and filled the dishwasher, and if he'd proved to his mum he'd been polite enough to his aunts, it did mean that the couple of hours afterwards would be his own.

As usual, his aunts arrived just in time for dinner and they were soon all sitting around the table, Johnny trying his best to use his cutlery properly. They were fixated about his fringe, which his mum half-heartedly defended. One of his aunts declared that it was scruffy, while the other one kept repeating how cute it made him look. He didn't know which was worse.

He kept zoning out of the conversation by thinking about the stranger who had saved him from Jordan. He was sure that the woman knew about them and their mission. What was the chance anyone else who was aware of the secret side of the museum would happen to be on the High Street just at the time Jordan found him? It all seemed too incredible when he tried to think about it logically, but logic had taken quite a battering over the last few weeks.

Eventually, dinner was over and Johnny had just switched on the dishwasher when there was a soft tap on the kitchen door. Yaz walked in. 'Merry Christmas Johnny.'

She went through to the dining room and after a few minutes of talking to his mum and aunts, and receiving glowing comments about how tall and well she looked, she was back in the kitchen.

'Perfect timing.' Johnny grabbed his dad's jacket and glanced at the clock, three o'clock. 'Let's go find Ted, he should be on his way over.'

Yaz was out the door first. 'Thank you for your present by the way.'

'Erm, glad you like it,' Johnny replied, realising he was blushing.

Yaz told him about her day, which involved lots of family and curries but no presents except for the ones from him and his mum. She said how much she liked the manga graphic novel he'd bought her. They spotted Ted ambling down the street towards them. He'd missed seeing Ted and was itching to persuade him to return to Egypt, but decided not to mention it. They were quickly talking about their presents. Ted's, as usual, were the most impressive, but he had only brought a code-breaking game with him. This was the first year Yaz had joined them on Christmas Day, but it felt sort of natural.

'Let's head down the park,' said Johnny.

They crossed the road and were soon in the park where they decided to break a code. Ted unfolded the board on a bench and stacked a set of cards next to it. He then took the first card and asked them questions, but Johnny and Yaz found it too hard, despite Ted telling them they were easy.

Yaz persuaded them to play tag, which involved Johnny and Ted swapping who was on as Yaz was too fast and kept creating new bases where she was safe. Johnny lunged towards Yaz, who leapt out of the way onto a balance beam when a loud booming noise shook the air and made the ground tilt. Yaz fell off the beam, crying out as she hit the ground. Another boom rolled across the sky and they looked at each other in shock.

'Sonic boom?' Johnny asked.

Ted shook his head. 'Wouldn't shake the ground. It's more like an earthquake, but that's almost impossible here.'

They heard it again, louder and closer. Johnny froze as he thought it sounded like the heartbeat he'd heard on their first day at High School, the day it had all started. The deep sound ebbed and flowed again and again as an increasingly louder double boom. This time, Yaz and Ted obviously could hear it too. They were motionless, mouths open.

'You can hear it?' Johnny looked at the sky to see if it was moving.

Ted nodded.

'What, what is it, Johnny?' Ted covered his ears and closed his eyes to try and block it out.

'This is what I was trying to tell you about at the start of the year.'

Yaz stood up and carefully tested her hurt ankle. 'Then we need to run.'

The sky started to bend out of shape above the houses by the side of the park, making their roofs move up and down as if they were breathing. Whatever it was, it was heading towards them.

'Come on,' shouted Johnny, gesturing to the far end of the park.

They jogged after him, but were only halfway across the large, open expanse of grass when Ted stopped. 'My code game!'

He turned and ran back to get it.

'No!' shouted Johnny. The rippling sky spread right over the park and reverberated to the deafening boom—boom, boom—boom, boom—boom.

'Stop, Ted,' called Johnny, but Ted was at the bench where he had left the game. A swirling wind came out of nowhere and Johnny smelled that musky, woody smell again. He watched in horror as Ted reached out for his game, only to see the cards shoot into the air one by one and twist around each other as if caught in a mini-tornado. Ted frantically groped after them, then slammed his hand down on the board as it began to lift up. The board's sides tugged and flapped, and Ted had to lean on it to stop it from flying away. As the cards spiralled higher, they disappeared into thin air one at a time, as if they simply winked out of existence. Ted froze, staring into the space where the cards vanished.

Johnny gasped as he saw the air in the same spot solidify into the shape of an arm and fist. He could still see clouds and sky through the arm, but they were distorted like the pattern on a shirt sleeve. Johnny's memory snapped back to the morning his trainer was snatched into thin air; this was identical. He felt pins and needles again, just as he had that day, as he watched the arm slowly reach down towards Ted. It looked like it was battling against some invisible force. The heartbeat echoed around the park, growing louder and louder as the hand extended downwards and uncurled its fingers.

'Come on Yaz.' Johnny sprinted forwards, carried by a surge of tingling energy. They each grabbed one of Ted's arms and pulled him away just as the hand broke free of its invisible shackles. It plunged into the space where Ted had just been and smashed into the bench with a thud that crumpled the game board into nothing. What sounded like a groan of exasperation resounded across the sky as Johnny and Yaz half-dragged, half-ran with Ted across the park. A gale threatened to push them over. Johnny risked a glance behind him, fearful that whatever it was would follow them, but the arm folded in on itself and disappeared.

They stood, chests heaving, staring around them in case the thing attacked them from somewhere else, but everything was silent and still once more.

'My game, what will mum and dad say?' Ted was distraught. 'I'll get into trouble for losing it.'

'I'm sorry.' Johnny put his hand on Ted's shoulder.

'But, it's worse than that,' Ted continued. 'You know what this means, don't you?'

Johnny looked at Ted, unsure what he was going to say.

Ted pointed to the space above the bench. 'That thing, that Shadow Lord or whatever Mr Merryweather calls it, it knows where we are, it can track us! We're not safe.' Ted moaned in anguish. 'Oh blast, it means the Curator is right, the barrier between dimensions is getting weaker. So...'

Johnny felt his hopes rise. 'So what Ted?'

'Aaaaaaaaah, this is so annoying,' shouted Ted at the sky. 'It means we do have to get the Golden Ankh. We actually have to go back to Ancient Egypt.'

Johnny let out a sigh of relief and grinned. This was the best Christmas present ever.

22

Back to Museum Club

Johnny brushed snow from his jacket and slumped in his chair on the first day of the new term. His mind was on tomorrow's Museum Club. He just had to keep his head down and hope Mr Leadbitter didn't pick on him during tutor time or P.E., though he wasn't that worried if he was given detention today. An hour or so after school cleaning sports equipment or writing lines wouldn't be the end of the world. He thought his luck was in when he made it to lunch break without incurring Mr Leadbitter's wrath, then a snowball hit him in the face. As he wiped away the cold slush, he could hear Jordan laughing. His anger snapped and he quickly scooped up some snow and crushed it into a snowball. The cold snow made his fingers tingle as he threw it at Jordan. It seemed to zip out of his hands like a bullet and smacked into Jordan's forehead with a sickening thud. Jordan fell backwards right into the arms of Mr Leadbitter, who had just walked around the corner.

'Armstrong, go to my tutor room now!' roared Mr Leadbitter, who then helped Jordan to the first aid room.

Johnny jumped as Mr Leadbitter stormed into his tutor room, banging the door behind him. 'You could have badly injured Jordan. What were you thinking of making a snowball around a pebble?'

'But, I didn't, sir,' replied Johnny. What was this all about?

'Then what do you call this?' Mr Leadbitter slammed a small, translucent pebble down on his desk. It looked like quartz.

Johnny tried to protest his innocence.

'Enough!' snarled the teacher. 'Detention tonight and no Museum Club tomorrow. Now get out of my sight.'

Johnny couldn't concentrate on any lessons for the rest of the day and when he told Ted the bad news he almost broke into tears. How could this happen, just when they were about to go back to Egypt after all this time?

Straight after the school bell, he trudged towards Mr Leadbitter's office for detention.

'Anything wrong Jonathon?' Mrs Corabella stopped him in the corridor and looked kindly at him.

Johnny explained what had happened and that Mr Leadbitter had banned him from Museum Club.

'I'm sure you didn't mean it, Jonathon. Did you?' Mrs Corabella held him in her birdlike gaze.

'No miss,' Johnny mumbled back.

'Well, you just leave it with me,' she smiled. 'You run along home and attend Museum Club tomorrow.'

Johnny hurried to leave the school as soon as he could.

'Oh, Jonathon, one more thing,' Mrs Corabella called after him.

He stopped in his tracks.

'I would love to hear about Museum Club soon. Friday, in my office, just after school please.'

'Yes miss,' said Johnny. There was something about the way she said this made Johnny suspicious she was on to them, but he was so relieved to go to Museum Club after all, that he soon forgot about it as he ran out of school.

* * *

Johnny, Ted and Yaz dashed into the museum, gobbled down toast and marmalade and left the Buxton Room with Mr Merryweather. Johnny spotted Alisha and Emily whispering to each other as they watched them leave. He didn't care, they were going to Egypt. As soon as they were out of the room, he talked excitedly with Yaz about where they would go and whether they would meet Tutankhamun again. Ted was talking more nervously with Mr Merryweather.

They were soon back in the Time Machine, where the Curator looked at them over his glasses. 'This visit is of vital importance, your most important one yet from what Ted has told me of your encounter with the Shadow Lord on Christmas Day. I fear we have little time remaining to recover the Golden Ankh. I hope, therefore, that you do not mind that Edward and myself have devised a plan.'

Johnny looked at Ted in surprise. A plan? He hadn't realised Ted was this enthusiastic about their return to Egypt.

The Curator continued, 'Edward has done some excellent research. We now think that there may be one of only two places where the Golden Ankh can be found. Edward has suggested an ideal time to retrieve it; would you do me the honour of explaining?'

Ted looked bashful as he spoke quietly. 'Yeah. So, it looks like Tutankhamun's death catches everyone by surprise. When he dies, the Grand Vizier snatches power over his rival, General Horemheb, but has to keep his plans secret and move fast to secure control. The only good thing about our last visit to Egypt was finding out

Tutankhamun likes to keep the Golden Ankh close to him. I think it is most likely by his throne in the palace at Karnak, which is next to Thebes. He said he also liked to show it off in his temple, that must be Luxor, which he paid to have repaired.'

Ted paused and looked at Mr Merryweather, who nodded. 'I agree with Edward. Focus on these two locations during your visit. There is another thing, is there not Edward?'

'It's not so nice.' Ted blew out his cheeks. 'I think the best time to visit is when Tutankhamun dies. That's another five years after we last met him. Everyone will be running around madly, and the Grand Vizier and the General should be facing off against each other. I hope there'll be chaos and we can use that as cover to get the Golden Ankh.' Ted's eyes lit up. 'And we'll be there when the most famous Pharaoh dies. How cool is that?'

'Won't it be, like, dangerous?' asked Yaz.

Ted blinked. 'Erm, yes. But I really hope they're all too busy to bother with us.'

Mr Merryweather interrupted, 'Well, as we're all happy with the plan, best get started to make the most of your time.'

They sat down in the armchairs, and Mr Merryweather set the date of the globe for what he estimated would be days before Tutankhamun's death, then he left the room with instructions to come right back if he had calculated the date incorrectly.

As the familiar swirling clouds gathered pace and lit the room with their orange glow, and the humming, vibrations and click-click-click of the numerals grew louder and faster, Johnny's mind raced away as he thought about their new adventure. He sort of agreed with Ted that it would be cool to be around when Tutankhamun died, but that also made him feel sad. Tutankhamun had seemed kind when they'd met him before and Johnny realised he liked him.

23

Break In at the Temple

This time, Ted led them through the streets of Thebes, following the same route toward the temple that they had taken before. Yaz hid her bag of snacks, water bottle and torch under her tunic. It was about an hour before dark and the sun was dipping low over hills around the Valley of the Kings. Ted's plan was to sneak into the temple as it became dark because there should be fewer people around. Johnny hoped Ted was right, they could have a look around, find the Golden Ankh and make it back to the Time Machine before Museum Club ended. He also wished to meet Tutankhamun one last time.

When they reached the temple, Ted started pacing along the wall, clearly searching for something.

'What are you looking for Ted?' asked Johnny.

'A door, a very small door. I've been looking at

the archaeological plans online and there is a narrow gap I think could be a door.' Ted kept pacing. 'It should be about … here!'

Ted stopped in front of a low, narrow gap hidden deep in the wall. It was easy to miss unless you knew where to look.

Yaz whistled in appreciation.

'Great find Ted,' said Johnny. 'Does it open?'

Ted pushed and pulled, but the door appeared stuck tight until, with a creak and groan, it swung suddenly in, dragging Ted with it. Johnny looked around to check no one was watching and ducked through the door, tripping over Ted, who was lying on the floor. Johnny landed in something soft and very smelly.

Yaz followed quickly and hauled Ted to his feet. 'I'm impressed, but, oh my god, what is the stink?' She took out her torch and they could see that they were in a narrow room ankle deep in feathers, bones and bird droppings. The ceiling was higher than the torch beam could reach. They could hear pigeons cooing in the darkness overhead.

Johnny stood up, his knees and hands covered in bird poo.

'Good grief, that smells rank,' said Ted holding his nose.

'You could have checked,' complained Yaz.

'Erm,' said Ted, wiping his hands on his clothes.

'As if this is going to appear on an archaeological plan of the temple.'

'Let's just get out of here before I'm sick,' said Yaz. 'Which way?'

'Let's see,' droned Ted, who was still holding his nose. 'We're actually inside the walls. There is a series of chambers that run right to the back of the temple. We just need to go through there to the next one.' Ted pointed at a low gap and gulped. 'Sorry guys.'

The gap was little more than knee height and they'd have to crawl through a stinking pile of dead birds and muck.

'Thanks, Ted, after you.' Yaz shone her torch on the gap and pushed Ted forwards. 'Your plan, so you get first turn in the bird poop.'

After what seemed like forever crawling from one poo-filled chamber to another, they came out into a large hall full of ornately carved, painted columns. They all stood up, stretched their backs, breathed deeply to clear their lungs of the acrid smell, and tried to shake off as many feathers and pigeon droppings as they could. Johnny thought they would look like some of the worst street urchins ever if anyone saw them. Luckily, the temple was in darkness and empty, just as Ted had hoped.

Rows and rows of red, yellow and blue painted

birds, eyes, ankhs and other patterns came in and out of view as Yaz swung her torch beam across one column after another. 'Where to now Ted?'

Ted reached into his tunic. 'Shine your torch over here.' It lit up a scrap of paper with the temple rooms outlined in black lines. 'If it is in the temple, I think the Golden Ankh will most likely be in a big hall called the Sun Court. It's where religious processions end. It was one of the best things we saw when we were on holiday so I bet it will look amazing now.'

Ted led them through the maze of columns and rooms until they came into a massive room lined with even more columns. 'It should be over here, where everyone would see it.'

Yaz swung her torch back and forwards a few times. It was empty and Ted's shoulders slumped in failure.

'Don't worry Ted.' Johnny felt disappointed but didn't want Ted to give up. 'Could it be somewhere else in the temple?'

Before Ted could answer, they heard a shout and the sound of running feet from the other side of the hall. They turned to see the hall flooded with flickering torchlight that created madly jumping giant shadows as guards poured in through a large door.

Shouts of 'seize them' echoed off the columns

and they were soon surrounded by soldiers pointing some nasty looking spears and curved swords at them.

'Shall we kill them now sir?' asked the nearest guard, who was thrusting his spear menacingly at Ted's chest.

'Hold on Khopesh,' barked the man who was obviously in charge. 'While I admire your enthusiasm, and I'm very tempted to, just because this lot have disturbed my sleep, we're under strict orders to take prisoners to the palace. Their majesties are short of slaves due to the plague. Bring them, and I may just return to my bed before dawn.'

'Not the plague again,' said Johnny as the guards shoved them towards the temple door.

24

To the Pharaoh's Palace

Johnny's first sight of Tutankhamun's palace was as a dark silhouette on the horizon, under a sky full of stars. They'd walked along the dusty Avenue of Sphinxes under the light of a half moon. His wrists hurt from where they were tied together. He was thirsty and hungry, his feet were sore, and his back ached from being constantly prodded with a spear shaft whenever he tried to talk to Ted or Yaz. They were surrounded by shifty-looking, well-armed guards, who seemed eager for an excuse to kill them. It wasn't really how he'd expected their mission to go. His mind raced with thoughts about what terrible things would happen to them when they reached the palace. He was feeling fairly positive that execution wasn't on his imaginary list, but he put imprisonment, beatings and starvation in the 'definite' column, with catching the plague again in 'highly likely'. They'd escaped dying from it on their last mission because of the First Aid Kit, but it didn't look like there'd be any chance of getting to the Time Machine quickly this time. At least Yaz had a bag full of chocolate and energy bars, so they'd not starve if their wrists were ever untied.

He tried asking Ted what the average life expectancy for an Ancient Egyptian slave was, but that question was cut off by another spear shaft in his back. He guessed the answer was short. He tried to forget about missing person reports on the news at home by thinking that the palace was the other place the Golden Ankh was likely to be. At least this got over the problem of how to break in.

They were soon pushed into an empty, tiny, foul-smelling stone cell. The door was slammed and bolted shut behind them, leaving them in pitch darkness.

Johnny stood motionless, not knowing what to do, while Ted groaned. Yaz sighed and turned on her torch, which made him jump.

'How did you do that?' asked Johnny, realising her hands were free.

'Easy, just rub and twist your wrists until the knots work loose,' she replied as she undid their ropes.

'Do you still have chocolate?' Asked Ted.

'I wish,' replied Yaz. 'I lost my bag crawling through the poo-filled walls of the temple.'

'Oh well.' Ted winced as he rubbed the rope burns on his wrists.

It took them just seconds to look around their cell. It was bare, windowless, smelled like a public toilet, and the door had no handle on their side.

'No way out of this one then.' Yaz squatted down on a relatively clean bit of floor. 'Hey, history boy, what did Egyptian slaves do?'

Ted sniffed. 'Anything they were told to. Breaking rocks, carving out tombs, building temples, serving food, cooking, cleaning.'

'Let's hope they don't forget we're here,' replied Yaz.

'Thanks for that cheery thought,' said Johnny as he sat down. They were stuck here until someone opened the door from the outside.

* * *

It was impossible to tell how long they'd been locked inside the cell when the door swung open and they were blinded by daylight.

'Come with us,' shouted the large figure silhouetted in the door.

They stumbled out of the cell, and were shoved into an outside courtyard where children and adults were milling about. A man with a shaved head sat at a table at one side of the yard. Johnny noticed he scowled a lot, and regularly flicked at flies with something that looked like a miniature whip made from animal hairs. For a brief moment, Johnny thought the man was Mr Leadbitter. Hunger must be making him see strange things.

Their guard pushed them to a halt in front of the man. 'Stand up straight for the Household Slave Supervisor,' he barked.

Johnny was relieved that their translators were still working. He didn't like to think what sort of punishment they'd get if they didn't immediately do what they were told.

They tried to straighten up, though they were stiff and cold from the stone cell.

The guard continued, 'These are the children that were found in the temple, sir.'

A thin, unfriendly, smile curled the edges of the supervisor's mouth and made him look even more like Mr Leadbitter. 'Saved from instant execution by the plague.' His voice was thin and reedy. 'No sign of coughing?'

'No sir,' replied the guard.

'A blessing,' whined the Supervisor. 'Send the Assyrian girl to the Queen's quarters. The Queen has lost so many attendants, she complains daily. As for these two, get them working in the kitchens.'

The Supervisor cracked his fly whip down hard on the table, which made Ted jump.

They were herded by the guard into the centre of

the yard. 'You girl,' he nodded to Yaz. 'Go to the women's dormitory. You two, follow me.'

Johnny and Ted washed in cold water, changed into slightly cleaner tunics and ate a breakfast that looked like porridge and beans but smelled and tasted of fish. It was disgusting but they were starving so they ate it anyway, until another slave snatched away their half-full bowls and led them into a maze of corridors that went deep into the palace. Johnny tried to remember where they turned from one corridor to another, but quickly lost track.

'Do you know the way back?' Johnny whispered to Ted.

Before Ted could reply, the slave prodded Johnny painfully between the shoulders with a wooden rod. 'Stop talking,' he grunted.

Johnny glimpsed Ted nod and hoped he was answering yes.

They came to a dark, hot, noisy room full of smoke, steam and people. The heat, cooking smells, clamour of voices, and sounds of chopping overwhelmed Johnny, who would have stopped at the door if their guard hadn't rammed the rod into his back again.

They had been sent to the kitchens; hot as a furnace and as noisy as a football crowd. Dozens of people were rushing between large benches, open fires and ovens, while others chopped meat and vegetables or stirred vast pots suspended over roaring fires. Orders were shouted across the room and people were constantly hurrying out through a wide door carrying steaming plates of food. Their guard pushed and poked them through the crowd, where they were shouted at for getting in the way, until they came to a door on the other side of the room and entered an open courtyard. It was full of long, low water troughs surrounded by kneeling boys scrubbing plates, bowls and pots. The courtyard was, mercifully, cooler and quieter than the kitchen, even though the sun was already beating down on them.

Their guard shouted at a lanky, brutish-looking older man, whose body was crisscrossed with scars. He was standing at one end of the long row of troughs. 'Hey, Narmer. New pot washers for you.' With that, he gave them one last push and disappeared back through the kitchen.

Narmer stared at them, fists on hips and a thick wooden rod gripped between two fingers. Johnny now recognised the rod as the favourite way for supervisors to punish slaves and guessed that Narmer used it enthusiastically.

'Right, you pair of foreign dung balls, get washing. No talking, no idling.'

Johnny couldn't see any space beside the troughs.

'Now!' Narmer stepped forward and raised his stick as if to hit them. Johnny pulled Ted down and they pushed their way between two other boys to begin scrubbing plates from a stack nearby.

25

Seth, God of Chaos

After what felt like hours scrubbing clay pots that made their knuckles red raw, Johnny and Ted watched the supervisor walk up to them accompanied by a short, fat man who had a mean expression and a whip. 'Merkha, here are those lads for you. They're as lazy as hippos so keep them working.'

'Come on you two, we've got the Pharaoh's daily food taxes to collect,' growled Merkha, snapping the end of the whip menacingly close to them.

They followed Merkha, who relaxed as soon as they were out of the courtyard. 'Sorry about the shouting and whiplashing boys, the palace supervisors expect it. Bullies, the lot of them. You look famished. That has bread and dates on top, help yourself.' He threw a sack for Johnny to catch and they dived in eagerly.

They soon reached a guarded door. Merkha

nodded at the soldiers, who opened it, and they were outside. Dozens of farmers formed a line that stretched away from the palace down towards the Nile. Each carried bundles of wheat, dates, fruit and vegetables.

'Their tax,' said Merkha. 'Just take the sacks from the one you're carrying, walk along the line and collect what they've brought.'

As Johnny reached the last farmer, the three sacks he was carrying were heavy and bulging. He felt sand sting his face and looked up to see a storm blowing towards them from across the Nile. Thick, dark clouds were piling one on top of the other, turning the distant desert grey under their shadow. The wind gathered speed and whipped up more sand. Merkha and the farmers noticed it too and they all looked worried as they started to pack up.

'Oh Horus, a sandstorm! Quick, let's get back to the shelter of the palace,' called Merkha as the flying sand grew thicker and louder. Within minutes it was dark and the palace disappeared from view. Merkha made them sit down, backs to the wind, but the swirling sand stung their faces, arms and legs. Johnny's bare arms and legs tingled where the sand was striking him and he thought he heard his heart thumping in his chest until he realised the sound was coming from the sky.

'Ted,' Johnny whispered. 'I've got that feeling

again, the one I got on Christmas Day and when I lost my trainer. I'm not sure, but it feels like there's something out there looking for me.'

Before Ted could reply, it grew darker, the wind roared and the palace roof tiles rattled. Just as quickly the sky cleared above their heads and the farmers shouted 'Seth, Seth!'

Johnny and Ted looked up to see a huge, dark beast like a fox or jackal with a forked tail swooping towards the palace. As it came nearer, it transformed into a man with a jackal's head, an Egyptian headdress billowing out behind it like a cloak. He extended his arms above his head; a staff appeared in one hand and an ankh in the other. He looked just like the god Seth painted inside the tomb they'd explored, and Johnny's stomach lurched as he tried to comprehend what he was looking at. A real Ancient Egyptian god was flying in the sky towards them. Had the farmers conjured Seth into being because of their fear of the sandstorm, or had the Shadow Lord created Seth and the storm? Johnny felt that Seth was searching for something or someone and watched in horror as the god's gaze swept closer to them. There was nowhere to hide.

Johnny felt hands grab his arms and realised Merkha was dragging them towards the palace. They disappeared inside just as Johnny glimpsed Seth's eyes stare down at him.

The sound of the gale was deafening even inside, and the guards looked petrified. Johnny could make out some of the words in the chaos, mostly, 'death' … 'destroy us' … 'disaster'.

'They believe Seth is making the storm,' said Ted as they followed Merkha, who was looking as scared as the guards.

'I saw him out there, Ted,' said Johnny.

Ted glanced back the way they'd come. 'I'd have said that was nonsense just a few weeks ago. Now, I don't know. If they believe the storm is being created by Seth then, I guess, they could manifest him just like Mr Merryweather said.' Ted shook his head. 'It's just too crazy.'

'Can you hear the sky booming, just like on Christmas Day?' asked Johnny. 'I think it's the Shadow Lord.'

Ted nodded. 'Makes sense, he's after the Golden Ankh. But if he can create the scariest god in Ancient Egypt it shows he's even stronger than Mr Merryweather thought. I don't like it at all.'

The storm eventually passed over the palace, the wind quietened down, and they were back in the dishwashing courtyard, where they were ordered to clean everything up. Everyone around them was agitated and said Seth was an omen of disaster. The supervisors shouted louder and whipped the more frightened slaves harder to keep control, but even they glanced nervously through the doors and at the roof as if they expected Seth to crash through the ceiling at any moment.

Johnny, Ted and some other boys were allowed back to the slaves' courtyard. Johnny's body ached and he was starving again. They hadn't eaten since breakfast, so he and Ted hurriedly gobbled down more of the gross cold, gloopy, fish-flavoured porridge they'd had at breakfast. Johnny longed for some of the chocolate and crisps in the Time Machine.

All the boys were on edge and glancing at the sky, now thankfully a calm dark blue. Johnny wanted to see Yaz as soon as possible, but she wasn't with the girls who entered the compound in pairs or small groups. They all sat down at an identical table behind Johnny and ate in silence. He glanced behind him. Nearly all the girls appeared to come from Africa or the Middle East and were probably between six and thirteen years old.

Johnny risked asking the boy next to him. 'Where are you from?'

The boy shook his head, before sneezing into his porridge.

Johnny felt the painful whack of a cane across his shoulders. 'No talking,' snarled a supervisor.

Just my luck thought Johnny, wincing.

The Grand Vizier strolled into the compound

with another important-looking man, who also had a shaved head, and eye make-up and wore gold bracelets. They walked slowly around the edge of the courtyard and waved away one of the supervisors. Johnny kept his head down in case Ay recognised him again. The two men whispered, heads bent together, and Johnny tried to listen to what they were saying. As he strained to hear, he felt the translator buzz as if tuning into their conversation for him. As they passed by, he heard just a few words, something about making the Pharaoh's special drink and joking how well the health tonic was working. They then left through separate doors.

The slaves were soon ordered to finish and lined up to wash their bowls in a communal sink, prayed for the departing Sun God Ra to return tomorrow morning, and for Tutankhamun's long life. Well, that's one thing that isn't going to happen, thought Johnny. The supervisors then left the compound and, almost immediately, everyone split into small groups of friends and sat around talking.

'At last,' exclaimed Johnny.

'I ache all over,' complained Ted, stretching his back.

'At least you haven't been beaten.' Johnny tried to look at the back of his shoulders as he carefully touched where he had been hit. It stung.

'Here, I can bathe it.' It was Yaz! Johnny tried to spin round to see her, but she held him still and gently placed a damp cloth on his back.

Johnny cried out, 'Ow!'

'It will help.' Yaz dabbed the cloth in a diagonal line across his shoulders. 'What did you find out?'

Johnny gritted his teeth against the stinging pain of water on his wound. 'We've seen Seth.'

'We heard. Everyone says it's an omen. The gossip is that it's a sign Tutankhamun is going to die. Soon.'

Johnny yelped in pain. 'Where have you been?'

'Tetchy, tetchy. You do want me to be gentle, don't you?' Yaz laughed, pressing the cloth harder. Johnny winced and, when the pain eased off, he nodded. 'Well, kitchen scrubbers, I've been with the Queen.'

Ted's jaw dropped. 'No way.'

'Yes way, Ted.'

'You're making it up,' Ted replied. 'There's no way they'd let a new slave be with the royal family on her first day.'

Yaz jabbed her thumbs towards herself. 'Well, they did with this slave. They must like me.'

'Or most of the palace slaves have died of the plague,' Ted snorted.

Yaz looked downcast. 'Yeah, maybe. They've lost over thirty this week. Watch out for people sneezing and coming out in boils. So I've been told.'

'Oh no,' exclaimed Johnny. 'The boy next to us at dinner sneezed.'

Yaz looked glumly at Ted. 'So, we might catch the plague again?'

'I hope not.'

'The First Aid Kit will save us again, though, won't it?' Johnny looked around to see if anyone else was sneezing.

'Only if we can get to it in time.' Ted looked worried. 'But it doesn't look like we'll get the chance.'

'We've been out once already,' said Johnny, trying to sound positive, 'so we know where one door is. I bet you can find your way back to where we collected the vegetables, can't you Ted?'

'Maybe,' said Ted thoughtfully, 'but it's guarded.'

'Can you sort them out with a few jujitsu moves Yaz?' Johnny felt a plan forming in his head.

'Easy, as long as they don't stab me with their spears first,' said Yaz, twirling her hands as if rehearsing a jujitsu move.

'What's the Queen like?' asked Ted. 'There aren't many records of her.'

'Queen Ankhesenamun is older and taller than King Tut, very snobby and really confident,' replied Yaz. 'She's also got, like, dozens and dozens of slaves. I was only the slave who helps the slave of the Queen's attendant.' Yaz paused, 'Oh and I met King Tut himself later too. High five?'

Johnny and Ted didn't raise their hands but gaped at her instead.

Yaz lowered her hand, looking embarrassed. 'Probably not appropriate in Ancient Egypt.'

'What's he like now?' asked Johnny.

'He's a right weedy teenager. Still doesn't look very mighty.'

Johnny leant closer to Yaz and whispered, 'Did you see the ankh?'

'Ha!' beamed Yaz. 'I wondered when you'd ask.'

'And?' Johnny and Ted shouted together, attracting glances from some of the others.

Yaz silently smiled at them and Johnny thought he was going to burst. Eventually, Yaz replied, her eyes twinkling. 'Yes, I've seen it.'

'Where?' asked Ted, looking nervously around him at the other slaves.

Yaz beckoned them closer still and whispered, 'In the Pharaoh's private rooms. It's just there, hung on the wall like a picture or something.'

Johnny stood up. 'Let's get it then.'

Yaz grabbed his arm and pulled him back down. 'Hold on. The palace is full of servants, guards and officials. I've seen the Grand Vizier strutting around like he owns the place and that Horemheb, the army general, skulking about with a face like thunder. When they're not with Tutankhamun, they're in the corridors arguing with each other, and when one goes to see Tutankhamun, the other tags along so he doesn't miss out on anything.'

'They're the ones who fight for power when Tutankhamun dies,' said Ted.

'I know that,' replied Yaz tetchy. 'I was there when Mr Merryweather told us.'

'I saw Ay when we were eating,' said Johnny. 'I heard him say something about the Pharaoh's special drink!'

Ted looked horrified. 'That must be poison.'

Johnny tried standing up again. 'We've got to save him!'

This time Ted seized his arm. 'Not so fast, Johnny. We can't change time remember? What has happened in the past has happened. Tutankhamun is meant to die because he died in our history.'

'He looks sick,' said Yaz. 'Seriously in need of a doctor.'

Ted looked hopeful. 'This could be our chance. We've four or five days left. If Tutankhamun dies within the next few days and everyone goes into meltdown as Ay and Horemheb battle it out, we have to grab the Golden Ankh and get it back to the Time Machine before Museum Club ends.'

Johnny felt sick at the thought of Tutankhamun's

death. 'What if we get the ankh and rescue Tutankhamun as well?'

'It's history Johnny, he's already died, thousands of years ago,' said Ted.

Johnny nodded, but he still didn't feel happy about a plan that included someone dying.

Ted continued, 'Can you find the Golden Ankh again Yaz?'

'Easy,' replied Yaz. 'I reckon we should check it out tonight.'

'Let's not rush into things.' Ted fidgeted with his ears.

'When?' Johnny liked the idea of getting back on their mission.

'After everyone is asleep,' said Yaz. 'I bet the security is rubbish.'

'OK, but it's just to look at.' Ted still looked worried. 'And we'll need a signal.'

Yaz patted her side. 'I've still got my torch. I'll shine it through your dormitory window after I've made sure no one's around.'

Johnny gave a thumbs up. 'No getting sneezed on, OK?'

26

The Palace by Night

Johnny had just about fallen asleep when Yaz's torch shone through the window and lit up the floor near his thin straw-filled mattress. Ted was already standing, so Johnny quietly joined him and they were soon following Yaz along darkened corridors into the palace.

'Ssssh.' Yaz stopped in front of two massive, wooden doors with gold handles and hieroglyphs inside an oval frame.

Ted ran his fingers over it. 'Tutankhamun's cartouche.'

'What is it then? I can see you need to tell us.' Yaz rolled her eyes.

'It's his name. The bird with the two bread loaves spells Tut.'

'Ha, so he really is King Tut!' laughed Yaz.

'The chequerboard, reed and wavy line are for the god Amun.'

'And the ankh is ankh, got it,' said Yaz impatiently. 'It gets better history boy. This is the actual door to the actual royal, actual apartment. The Golden Ankh is hanging on a wall in here. Once we're inside we might meet someone, but there's loads of bling furniture to hide behind. Just keep quiet and follow me. OK?'

Johnny and Ted nodded. Yaz pushed one of the heavy doors open, switched her torch off, then slipped through the gap. Ted went next and Johnny followed, quickly looking behind him. The corridor they had walked down was still empty.

They were at the edge of a large room, dimly lit by oil lamps. It was full of strange shapes and shadows and as Johnny's eyes got used to the dark, he could see that most of the shapes were ornate gold chairs, tables and statues. He was sure he recognised some of them from their visit to Tutankhamun's tomb in 1922. There were doors midway down the walls on either side and, in pride of place on the far wall, was the Golden Ankh. It was unguarded!

'This way,' whispered Yaz as she led them straight towards the ankh.

'Who is there?'

They all froze and looked at each other in shock. The words were softly spoken as if said by someone finding it a great effort to speak.

'I said, who is there?'

The voice came from slightly behind them and they all turned around to peer into the shadows. Johnny could just make out a long couch. A thin, gangly figure slowly and painfully leant up on one elbow. It was a boy a few years older than them, about school leaving age, with a shaved head and smudged eye make-up. He looked as if he'd been crying. Yaz dropped to her knees and bowed, arms outstretched. 'It is only us your highness, humble palace slaves, checking all is well.'

This was Tutankhamun! Johnny didn't recognise him. The Pharaoh leant against an arm of the couch, he was clearly struggling to stay upright.

'You, it is you again!' Tutankhamun stood up. 'I have been waiting for you. Horus has told me you are sent to save me from Ay.'

Yaz went to his side. 'Are you all right, erm, my lord?'

'See,' Johnny whispered to Ted. 'We have to do something now.'

Tutankhamun took hold of Yaz's hands. 'I am sure Ay is trying to kill me. Will you help? Is Horus right?'

'Yes he is and yes we can,' blurted Johnny. He thought, this is weird, but it's pretty cool to save a famous Pharaoh.

'No way,' said Ted through gritted teeth. 'Not on

the cards.'

'We can get him to the Time Machine,' insisted Johnny, who wasn't going to give up now. 'If he disappears then it's just the same as him dying. Ay will take over but Tutankhamun doesn't have to die.'

Ted shook his head. 'No, no, no. Don't you listen? There'll be no body in the tomb, no greatest news story of the 1920s, no amazing museum in Cairo, and no one will study how he died. This could end up with anything happening in the future.'

'Johnny's right, you know, we can't let the Grand Vizier kill him.' Yaz scrunched her face in torment.

'And how will we get out of the palace exactly?' Ted threw his arms up. 'With all the guards and no way of knowing where to go?'

'I can show you a secret way.' Tutankhamun looked hopeful. 'Really I can.'

'Can we get back to Thebes without anyone seeing us?' asked Johnny.

'I think so.' Tutankhamun scratched his head. 'If we go now, while it is dark.'

'OK,' said Yaz, 'we have to do this.'

Ted shook his head. 'This really isn't right. We're just looking around tonight, remember?'

'We need to bring the Golden Ankh.' Johnny was not going to listen to Ted. The chance to get the ankh and rescue Tutankhamun from assassination was too good to miss.

Tutankhamun looked toward the ankh. 'You are here to fulfil the prophecy?'

'What prophecy?' asked Ted.

'The one that states that the Golden Ankh will stop Seth from destroying the world if the boy Pharaoh works with the foreigners. It is in a secret scroll passed down to me by my father Akhenaten. I was hoping I would be that boy Pharaoh, but I had given up on seeing you again before Ay killed me.'

Johnny's heart pounded. This was getting even more strange, but it flicked a switch in his mind. What they had to do became very, very clear. 'Right, Tut … erm … your lord. We're going to get the Golden Ankh, then you can lead us out of your palace.'

Tutankhamun managed a weak grin. 'Of course. I need my stick. Oh, thank you Horus.'

Yaz turned on her torch. 'Let's take the ankh and go.'

'This is not good, not good at all,' said Ted. 'He really is poisoned.'

'We have to save him,' exclaimed Johnny.

'No way,' snapped Ted. 'We can't change time.'

'But, he'll die,' said Johnny, 'and we're part of a prophecy.'

'He's meant to die,' replied Ted, getting

frustrated. 'This is our past, not our present time.'

Johnny was about to shout at Ted when they heard angry voices behind the door to their right.

'Sssh you two.' Yaz squatted down.

'Oh, we're going to get ourselves killed.' Ted hid behind a table.

'Not if we just move.' Johnny headed for the Golden Ankh. 'Shine your torch on the ankh, Yaz.'

'I don't think so,' replied Yaz, who was frozen to the spot.

Her torch illuminated wisps of mist that were gathering together from all corners of the room and forming into a shape that quickly became solid.

'So we meet again.' The Sphinx sat like a cat curled up on its owner's lap but with a scowl on his face. 'What are you meddling children up to now?'

'Now what, you're Scooby Doo all of a sudden?' said Yaz as they backed away.

'Oh, don't think you can escape again, not this time. I will set you a harder riddle, one you have no hope of solving.'

'Horemakhet,' exclaimed Tutankhamun. 'Have you come to guide us?'

'Oh don't be silly little boy Pharaoh,' sneered the Sphinx. 'You don't have much time left if I can be honest with you. I am more interested in these three interlopers.'

The Sphinx stretched out as he stood up and

began to walk in a circle. He stopped by a table and conjured an hourglass out of thin air.

Johnny looked at Ted, who had solved the riddle in the temple during their first visit. Ted clenched his jaw in determination.

'We're ready,' said Johnny.

The Sphinx flipped the hourglass over with a claw and the sand began trickling down into the empty chamber.

'Answer me this. If you answer it correctly I will leave, but if you cannot solve it before the sands of time run out, you are coming with me.' With that, the Sphinx drew to his full height.

'I never was, am always to be,
No one ever saw me, nor ever will
And yet I am the confidence of all
To live and breathe on this earthly ball.
What am I?'

'Can you solve it, Ted?' Johnny kept his eyes on the Sphinx. He didn't trust him, remembering how angry he had been when they escaped the first time.

Ted was silent, lost in thought.

'Come on Ted,' urged Yaz.

'Shhh,' he replied, 'give me a minute.'

'Ah, time,' replied the Sphinx, tapping the hourglass with a smirk. 'Something you have precious little of.'

Almost half of the sand was now in the bottom of the hourglass. Ted was muttering to himself, his forehead scrunched into a frown. 'There could be so many answers to this one.'

Johnny watched the sand pour through the narrow gap in the middle of the hourglass, sure it was speeding up. Come on Ted, he thought. He didn't have a clue what the riddle's answer could be. Everything was up to Ted.

'I, erm, I think I have it.' Ted sounded more hopeful than certain.

The Sphinx arched an eyebrow. 'Oh really? You think you have the answer, do you? Only think? I would find it rather bothersome if you have. Still, let us hear your pearl of wisdom.'

Ted cleared his throat.

'Well, I've thought of all the possible answers, and almost said oxygen but, then I remembered what time we are in so…' Ted glanced nervously at Johnny and Ted as if asking for their forgiveness if he was wrong.

'Oh do hurry up,' complained the Sphinx. 'The sands are falling to their conclusion.'

The bottom of the hourglass was over three-quarters full.

'Here goes, wish me luck.' Ted looked at Johnny, Yaz and Tutankhamun, then stared once again at the

Sphinx. 'The answer is tomorrow.'

There was a moment of stillness, and then the Sphinx howled with rage and prowled around the room, scattering furniture and ornaments to either side. Johnny's heart leapt for joy, Ted must be right, but then he cowered as the Sphinx raced up to them. Perhaps it was going to kill them after all.

The Sphinx stopped eyeball to eyeball with Johnny as it leant its forehead against his, glowering and panting. Its breath smelled, distractingly, of fish.

'Your friend has saved you again,' it spat. 'A lucky guess, no doubt. I would so love to kill you, but I am bound by my stupid oath. Do not think this is the last you will see of me.'

With a final snarl, the Sphinx stalked around in a tight circle, like a cat trying to find a comfortable bed, then faded away in a whirl of evaporating mist.

Johnny and Yaz just had time to pat Ted on the back when they heard more voices, and the sound of running feet, outside the door to their right.

'Guards!' said Yaz. 'Quick.' She dashed towards the Golden Ankh.

27

Tutankhamun and the Golden Ankh

The doors burst open as servants and guards spilled through the door. Within seconds, the room was in chaos. Everyone was shouting or screaming, the guards were fighting with each other, and Johnny could hear people wailing that Tutankhamun was dead.

'Ted, hide Tutankhamun!' shouted Johnny. He saw them dive under a large couch beside the door on the opposite side of the room, while he and Yaz ducked behind a statue of Horus.

Johnny realised how close they were to the ankh, but now they had to find a way through the squabbling guards and panicking servants. Some servants grabbed small gold ornaments as they ran past and one or two guards tried to stop them in between fighting each other. Johnny was worried

that someone might take the ankh and he tapped
Yaz on the hand to signal she should follow him.
They snaked their way between the fleeing and
fighting people towards the wall where the Golden
Ankh gleamed down at them. Johnny hoped the
fighting continued long enough for them to get the
ankh and get out. They were soon by the wall but
the ankh was too high to reach so Johnny picked up
a chair and stood on it. He was sure he'd attract
attention as he reached up, took the ankh in both
hands and gently pulled. It came away from the wall
more easily than he expected and he almost fell
backwards under its weight. He swayed on the chair
for a second before regaining his balance.

Johnny let out a sigh of relief then went rigid
with fear as he heard a shout from the next room
carry above the din.

'Get the Golden Ankh you fools. Once I have it,
Horemheb cannot challenge me for the throne. His
men will be sure to change sides.'

Ay! Johnny thought quickly, what could he do?

'Here!' called Yaz.

Johnny glanced down to see her hiding behind a
large wooden cabinet that had fallen at an angle
against the wall. She held her arms up so he slid the
ankh to her then jumped. He landed lightly on the
floor and scrambled under the cabinet just as a
group of soldiers marched up to the chair he'd been

standing on a second earlier.

'The ankh has gone,' shouted the soldier leading them. 'By Horus, Ay will have us killed for this.'

Another gang of soldiers ran through the door next to the couch where Ted and Tutankhamun were hiding. 'Seize the traitors, they must have the Golden Ankh!'

The two groups met in a clash of swords and spears right beside the cabinet Johnny and Yaz were hiding under. Yaz gestured for Johnny to follow her to the other end of their hiding place, where she wrapped the ankh in a large piece of cloth. Bent over with the weight of the ankh, Yaz dashed towards the door the second group of soldiers had just come through. The dark room and chaos of the fighting soldiers made it easier for Yaz to get there than Johnny dared hope and she was soon out of the room. Johnny stopped to look for Ted and Tutankhamun as he passed by the couch. They weren't there! He hesitated, but a spear smashed into the couch with a sickening thump and he flung himself through the doors after Yaz.

'What now?' asked Yaz.

'Have you seen Ted and Tutankhamun?' replied Johnny.

Yaz shook her head and his heart sank.

'Where are they?' asked Johnny.

'Over here,' whispered Ted. He was looking

through another door on the far side of the room.

Johnny and Yaz grabbed the ankh and ran to the door as fast as they could, while Ted held it open for them. They were in a corridor and Ted was with a sheepish looking Tutankhamun, dressed as a girl with a shawl over his head.

'What now?' asked Ted nervously.

'We have to get out,' said Yaz.

'That's obvious,' moaned Ted. 'How?'

'We are near the secret way,' said Tutankhamun, who led them to a statue of a cat standing against the wall, where he disappeared.

'What?' said Johnny in disbelief.

'Follow me,' called Tutankhamun from behind the statue. His slender hand reappeared and beckoned them to him.

'Come on.' Johnny picked up the ankh and led them behind the statue where they found a hidden door. Tutankhamun was a few steps down a dark, narrow passage that was obviously hidden within the wall between two corridors.

Yaz switched on her torch again and they followed Tutankhamun. The Pharaoh's bad leg and the effects of the poison slowed him down more than Johnny liked. Eventually, they reached a small door and Tutankhamun carefully opened it to reveal a small courtyard. It was rapidly filling with people, who were surging along a wide corridor towards an open door between two statues of Tutankhamun. Slaves, servants and priests were scrabbling and pushing to escape. Some were bleeding from wounds and two women were carrying an unconscious friend by the arms and legs. A small group of well-dressed important-looking people were trying to force their way through, but they were constantly shouted at and beaten back. Johnny assumed they must be court officials fleeing from Ay. The atmosphere was getting ugly, as tempers flared and the crowd crushed together at the door. Johnny was sure someone would recognise their Pharaoh as they quietly entered the courtyard but, so far, no one was looking their way.

Tutankhamun sighed. 'Perhaps it is not as secret as I had hoped.'

'Everything's, like, broken down, just as Mr Merryweather said.' Ted sounded amazed at the Curator's prediction. 'How could he know? Nothing like this is ever recorded in books about Ancient Egypt.'

'Let's leave the history until we're home,' said Yaz.

Johnny stared at the crowd. 'It's going to take ages to get out. We'll never make it without being caught.'

Yaz tugged at his sleeve and pointed at the far side of the courtyard, beyond the mass of people.

The Grand Vizier stood at the head of a group of soldiers and he was searching the crowd for someone. Johnny ducked down but Ay spotted them and shouted orders at his men, who started to fight their way through the crush.

'We're not getting out this way,' said Johnny. 'Anywhere else?'

Tutankhamun was about to say something but Yaz interrupted him. 'I'm sure I was here yesterday. King Tut, isn't there another door somewhere nearby?'

'There is a large door with statues of Isis, but it will be busy too,' said Tutankhamun.

'That's it,' replied Yaz. 'It has to be better than running into Ay.' She pushed against the throng of people heading towards the door to thread her way along the corridor they were pouring out of.

Ay shouted at them. 'You have something that belongs to me. Stop in the name of your Pharaoh.'

'He's not wasted any time,' shouted Ted. 'We're all dead if he catches us.'

'Keep your head down,' Yaz said to Tutankhamun as she pushed him in front of her. 'Here.' Yaz disappeared down an empty corridor to their right.

Johnny, Ted and Tutankhamun followed but Johnny didn't fancy their chances of escaping the Grand Vizier's soldiers. He was struggling to run with the ankh, Ted's asthma was getting worse and Tutankhamun was limping badly. Johnny could hear the soldiers gaining on them and he began to feel so desperate that he felt the urge to throw the ankh into one of the rooms as they ran past but he couldn't let go.

'Here we are,' shouted Yaz, turning to them with a smile.

They entered another courtyard, much larger than the one they'd come from, in front of a wide door between statues of Isis that led outside. It was also full, but there was more space than where they'd come from, so people weren't as crushed together. Two groups of soldiers were fighting to their right. One was led by General Horemheb, who was winning.

'Quick,' said Yaz. 'Let's disappear into the crowd.'

Yaz dragged Tutankhamun into the knot of people heading towards the door. Johnny slipped in beside her, while Ted stumbled in behind them. Johnny glanced back through the heads and faces crowding around to see the Grand Vizier and his men arrive in the courtyard. They came come to an abrupt halt when they saw Horemheb and his men, who pushed through the few remaining opponents to charge in Ay's direction. The Grand Vizier shouted in frustration as he and his soldiers quickly turned to defend themselves.

Johnny didn't know how they did it, but they managed to squeeze, wriggle and worm their way through the bodies, arms and legs between them and the door until they were outside. He was relieved that no one recognised Tutankhamun, who looked convincingly like a girl, but Yaz had to stop him ordering people to make way for their Pharaoh at one point. She said they probably didn't care, wouldn't believe him and all he'd do was give them away to the men with the sharp swords. Tutankhamun went very quiet and obedient after that.

The night air was cool and fresh, and the moon provided just enough light to see the way along the Avenue of Sphinxes. It was rammed with people fleeing to Thebes. They disappeared into the crowd and Johnny dared to believe they were actually going to get away.

28

Race to the Time Machine

Johnny started to get nervous as dawn lightened the sky and the sun rose to flood the Avenue with morning light. It had been easy to hide in the crowd during the dark, while everyone carried bags, baskets and bundles wrapped in cloth, but he was sure someone would recognise Tutankhamun in daylight. He became jumpier and jumpier the closer they got to Thebes as people went down side streets and the crowd thinned out. Someone started to shout in front and Johnny craned his neck to see who it was.

'Soldiers,' whispered Yaz. 'Hide King Tut behind us.'

The crowd parted to reveal a line of soldiers straddling the Avenue, with Ay shouting commands from the centre. Soldiers were grabbing, questioning and searching everyone who wanted to get past or was too slow to disappear into a side street. The men emptied large bags and baskets, and Johnny knew they were looking for the Golden Ankh. There was no way they could hide it or Tutankhamun from the guards.

'We're done for,' whimpered Ted.

Johnny searched around desperately for a way out and noticed the cluster of ramshackle buildings with its warren of alleys that they had gone into during their first trip to Egypt. The soldiers were more interested in the Avenue and the wider side streets that led away from the river. The alleys looked unguarded.

'Quick, in here,' hissed Johnny and he ran towards the nearest alley. Ted and Yaz followed but were slowed down trying to help Tutankhamun limp along. He was going as fast as he could but had slowed down as the night wore on towards morning. He was also clearly ill. They were almost at the alleyway when they heard a shout.

'Stop where you are,' ordered Ay, directing a group of soldiers in their direction.

Everyone near them scattered in all directions, screaming, dropping bags and getting in each other's way, which luckily slowed down the soldiers.

'Hurry up.' Yaz shoved Tutankhamun ahead of her.

Johnny ran as fast he could carrying the Golden

Ankh, his stomach lurching as it almost slipped from his grasp. He stumbled, nearly bringing down Ted, but Yaz caught him by his arm and pulled him into the dark and cool alleyway.

'Where's the safest way out?' Yaz asked Tutankhamun.

'I, I do not know.' Tutankhamun looked crestfallen. 'I have never been in here before.'

'Of course not. What was I thinking of? Keep running everybody,' called Yaz. 'We'll go left then right at every corner.'

They zig-zagged through the narrow alleys, turning over tables and kicking over stacks of clay pots as they ran. They even sent a small herd of goats bleating in all directions. Strangely, no one came out to confront them, as if everyone was lying as low and quiet as possible. Johnny was scared that the noise would attract the soldiers, but at least there was no one to recognise Tutankhamun. They were deep into the alleyways when Johnny heard shouts and he glanced back to see soldiers filling the far end of the alley behind them. They were nearly at a little crossroads and Yaz went to the left. Johnny hauled the ankh around the corner and crashed straight into the back of her. She had skidded to a halt in front of the Grand Vizier and another group of soldiers. Ted and Tutankhamun caught up with Johnny.

'Give yourselves up, children.' Ay stepped

forward. 'You are trapped and have something I want.'

His chest heaving for breath, Johnny stared silently and wide-eyed at the Grand Vizier. Yaz and Ted backed away, with Tutankamun hidden behind them. They were stuck. Johnny felt the prickle of tears again. How did Ay know to find them here?

Ay smiled and slowly walked towards them. 'You know what I mean, give me the Golden Ankh.'

Johnny couldn't move, sensing every angle and edge of the ankh as it pressed into him. He did not want to hand it over after everything they'd gone through.

Ay let out a long sigh. 'Do not fool with me, boy. I do not know why you want the ankh, but this is not your war. Your little game is up. I now have the Golden Ankh and its power will make me Pharaoh. I can do away with that scheming, lying, deceitful Horemheb at last. Hand over the ankh or I will cut it from you.'

Ay drew a lethal-looking curved sword, pointed it at Johnny's chest, and held out his other hand as he took another step forward. Johnny was frozen to the spot. It was obvious that there was no way out and the Grand Vizier's men would kill them whatever he did, but he couldn't believe they had come to the end of the road. Anger and sadness welled up from deep inside him; he felt his stomach churning and his heart pounding. His mum's face swirled into view and he realised how upset she'd be, that she would miss him when he didn't come home. Guilt poured over him as he thought about how he'd led Ted and Yaz to their deaths and, despite this, they still stood beside him. It was so, so unfair that it made his head buzz.

The buzzing changed into the sounds of splintering and crackling. Someone shouted 'Fire!' and the alley filled with heat and smoke.

'By Sekhmet, damn Horemheb,' coughed Ay.

Johnny felt someone grab his arm, he tried to resist but was quickly pulled off-balance and tumbled sideways. He instinctively closed his eyes as he expected a sword or spear to smash into him. Instead, he fell into something warm and wet.

'Urgh, a toilet,' exclaimed Ted.

Johnny opened his eyes to see Ted and Tutankhamun sprawled beside him on the damp floor of a small room. He could hear the Grand Vizier shout and curse in the alley. A thin wall of dried reeds was all that separated them. Yaz had smashed through the reed wall on the opposite side.

'Up,' urged Yaz.

They scrambled to their feet, their legs and arms damp with a foul-smelling liquid, and followed Yaz into a dark room with a rectangle of light ahead. A door, onto another street!

They were outside, thankfully in an alleyway empty except for a thick rain of ash and sparks.

'Out of the frying pan and into the fire.' Ted held his hand up to his mouth and coughed.

'Like, yeah,' said Yaz.

They staggered along the alleyway into thicker and thicker smoke. The roar of the fire and crackle of burning reeds surrounded them and they began to choke. Tutankhamun collapsed to his knees and Yaz picked him back up. He was clearly very weak and muttered 'Leave me.' No way, thought Johnny, who tried to stop the urge to panic about being trapped by the fire. He glanced around him for an escape route. Big clouds of smoke billowed down a lane to their right, where flames soared high above the rooftops. To the left, Johnny could see the sky and a clear run, so he set off towards the open air. They were almost at a wider road near the temple when a door of a building to his right swung open and blocked their way. Johnny ran smack into it and staggered backwards. A familiar silky voice called to them from the shadows inside the doorway.

Johnny groaned as the Sphinx stepped outside and sniffed the air. 'I sense someone has been busy and, I'd guess, they are not having a barbecue.' He turned his attention to them. 'So, I hear that Tutankhamun is dead. Long live the Pharaoh. But, who will it be? So you've abandoned Tut. No doubt he is being embalmed as we have our little chat, while two of his less-than-delightful sycophants slug it out over who fills his shoes. For what it's worth, and it is worth quite a bit, my money is on the Grand Vizier. He's far more ruthless than the General. Whoever put Horemheb in charge of the army didn't realise he couldn't fight his way out of a sack of figs. Anyway, I see you have a new friend, how charming.'

Tutankhamun started to speak but Yaz shook her head and put her finger to her mouth as she stepped forward and took up a fighting pose. Yaz is right, thought Johnny, it is better that the Sphinx doesn't know we have Tutankhamun.

The Sphinx turned his full attention on Yaz. 'Really, do you think you can threaten me?' He pointed a paw at his chest. 'I do not fall over easily. It is the four legs you see. They all come with claws, so don't push it.'

'What do you want?' Johnny asked desperately, one eye on the advancing flames.

'Oh, I think you know me by now, Jonathon,' purred the Sphinx.

'What? How do you know my name?' Johnny forgot the fire for a second.

'My dear,' the Sphinx smiled, 'thank you for confirming my suspicions. I did have a teensy little thought that you were not from here or this time, so

I did a spot of research and a little bird told me you had come from out of the blue to take one of the Pharaoh's trinkets. I guess you're trying to hide it under that rag there.' The Sphinx pointed a claw at the wrapped Golden Ankh. 'It turns out to be quite a popular ornament and one I may prefer to keep myself.'

'You're working for the Shadow Lord?' Johnny found himself fighting to breathe, either due to the smoke or a panic attack.

'I wouldn't go that far, as impressive as he seems. However, I do know one or two interested parties who would simply adore the Golden Ankh.' The Sphinx rose up on its hind legs and leant one arm against the door frame. 'Which means, it is riddle time again. If you can't answer the riddle correctly, I get to keep the treasure.'

'And if we're right?' Ted croaked with worry.

'Sadly, I'll have to let you go on your way as before.' The Sphinx scratched behind one of his ears.

'With the Golden Ankh?' asked Johnny.

'Indeed, with the Golden Ankh,' sighed the Sphinx. 'That is, sadly, part of the Sphinx code of honour you see. It can be a damn nuisance and a real shame in this instance. We're all bound by our destinies, are we not Jonathan?'

'What about Tutankhamun?' Johnny blurted out before he could stop himself.

The Sphinx looked wearily at Tutankhamun and slowly applauded. 'You mean your friend here is the Pharaoh? Oh, how delightful. I wonder whether either of the two pompous dimwits thought you would try to rescue him. To be honest, I have little interest in such a fleeting and trivial Pharaoh as this one here.'

The flames and smoke crept closer and Johnny looked at Ted. 'Are you ready to answer one more riddle?'

Ted swallowed and wiped away falling ash from his forehead. 'Haven't got much choice, have I?'

Johnny shook his head and put his hand on Ted's shoulder. 'Whatever happens, you've got us this far. So have you, Yaz. Ted, if you get this right we're almost home and dry, if you can't get it, don't worry.'

'OK Johnny.' Ted took a breath in and turned to the Sphinx. 'Go on then.'

'All very heart warming, I'm sure,' sniffed the Sphinx, 'but now you'll have to try your luck at this riddle and I've made it just a smidgen more difficult than the last one. Are you ready?'

Ted nodded.

The Sphinx theatrically cleared his throat,

'Only one colour, but not one size,
Stuck at the bottom, yet easily flies.

Present in sun, but not in rain,
Doing no harm, and feeling no pain.
What is it?'

Ted's jaw dropped, 'But that's impossible.'

'Good.' The Sphinx chuckled as he settled down on all fours again. 'Difficult yes, impossible no. Do you think I would make the riddle easy the third time around?' Yet again, he produced the hourglass out of thin air, its sands already flowing into the bottom chamber. 'However, your time is draining away, so, less chatter and more thinking my dear boy.'

'You can do it, Ted, I know you can,' Johnny encouraged softly.

Ted glared back at Johnny. 'I have no idea. I'm really sorry.'

'Go on Ted, think,' said Yaz.

'Oh, what can it be, what can it be?' muttered Ted, covering his face with his hands.

Johnny looked on helplessly and saw Yaz staring at the hourglass as if willing the trickle of sand to slow down. A trick of the light made it look like the grains of sand were suspended in midair. 'Cheeky,' growled the Sphinx, who swiped a paw at the hourglass and the illusion was shattered. The sand flowed faster through the narrow neck between the two chambers. The bottom of the hourglass was soon a quarter full. The fire was burning closer and Johnny could feel the occasional hot spark burn his skin. Ted didn't look close to an answer and Johnny was desperate to help but knew he had to keep quiet so as not to break his friend's concentration. His mind raced between Ted, the flames, his mum, Mr Merryweather, not returning home and failure. Just a third of the sand remained in the top chamber. Johnny heard shouts over the roar of the flames and wondered if Ay was searching for them beyond the fire.

Less than a quarter of the sand remained in the top now. A burning building crashed into the alley and sent a shower of sparks into the air. Ted didn't even notice, which Johnny hoped was a good sign. Maybe he was close to working out the riddle, right?

Johnny was transfixed by the last few grains of sand as they rolled around the top of the narrow opening to the bottom chamber before falling. He counted each of the remaining grains — 10, 9, 8, come on Ted, 7, 6, 5, you can do it, 4, 3, 2…

'Got it, maybe.' Ted looked petrified. 'The answer is a shadow?'

The last grain of sand seemed to hang in mid air, then dropped.

The Sphinx howled, his face ablaze with anger and he reared on his hind legs, towering above them as if to strike. Johnny dived to the floor with his hands over his head. When the blows didn't land, he looked up. The Sphinx was gone and the gate across the end of the alley fell backwards, crashing to the ground in a shower of dust and sand.

29

Battle of the Gods

Johnny blinked smoke from his eyes. 'Ted, you've done it, we're free.'

Yaz high-fived a drained-looking Ted, and was about to do the same to Tutankhamun but he just looked blankly at her.

The crackling of flames ended their celebrations, so Johnny hoisted the shrouded Golden Ankh over his shoulder, and they stepped out of the alley.

'The Time Machine is just around the temple, it's not far,' coughed Ted.

'What is the Time Machine?' Tutankhamun stood rooted to the spot.

'Your escape route, come on.' Johnny set off along the mercifully empty street towards the back of the temple.

'It looks like another storm,' said Yaz and they all looked up. The sky was quickly filling with fast-moving clouds and a breeze began to make the smoke and ash swirl around.

Johnny's shoulders drooped. 'Not Seth again?'

'Looks like it.' Ted pointed across the Nile to the mountains around the Valley of the Kings. Darker and darker clouds were piling on top of each other above the Valley, before spreading out like long fingers towards them. Flashes of lightning lit up the clouds and the breeze turned into a strong wind that made the fire crackle faster and louder.

'That is Seth?' Tutankhamun's voice quavered. 'It cannot be, he does not manifest himself like that.'

'Well, he does now.' Johnny broke into a trot. 'Yaz, help me with the ankh.'

Yaz grabbed one end of the bundle and they ran out of the alleyway to the road beside the temple. Ted was now wheezing loudly and Tutankhamun limped as fast as he could but was falling further behind. The buildings opposite the temple were a deafening, raging inferno, flames and thick smoke poured high into the sky and Johnny felt the heat rebound off the temple wall. They would have to move fast or they'd be cooked alive.

Johnny kept glancing upwards and saw the jackal-headed god hovering in the centre of the storm clouds. The god flew across the sky and was gaining on them fast, dark billows of clouds erupting in his wake. The deep booming of a heart echoed around the sky, even louder than the fire, and was punctuated with cracks of thunder and blinding lightning flashes.

'It is Seth!' Tutankhamun stopped again. 'There is no hope.'

'Of course there is,' yelled Yaz. 'Just get a move on.'

'We've got to get you and the Golden Ankh to safety.' Johnny felt he was begging Tutankhamun. 'Before Ay gets us.'

This spurred the Pharaoh to limp after them as best he could, and they reached the streets leading to the Time Machine. Seth was gaining on them and growing to a monstrous size. He spread his arms in front and a spear appeared in his right hand. Seth craned his grotesque doglike head from side to side, and Johnny's spirits rose a little. Seth didn't know where they were.

A deafening roar shook the ground and they saw a vast pillar of cloud erupt from the temple roof to solidify into a giant hawk-headed man holding a spear.

'Horus!' shouted Tutankhamun. 'Blessed Horus. Now Seth will be vanquished.'

'This can't be happening,' wheezed Ted.

Horus planted his feet on either side of the temple roof and raised his spear in front of him to face Seth. Johnny knew they should continue running, but they crouched down in a doorway to watch the god fight as Seth flew into Horus. Their spears clashed and a terrifying sound rent the sky, shaking the ground and sending stones cascading down from the temple roof. A column collapsed in a shower of dust.

Johnny, Ted and Yaz watched mesmerised as the two gods fought in the air, thrusting their spears, parrying attacks and circling each other. Each blow shook the ground and Johnny felt everything could break at any moment. Horus was slowly pushing Seth back across the Nile when a giant lion-headed woman leapt from the river in a cascade of water and lunged at Horus. She caught him by surprise, biting hold of his legs. He twisted in agony, and then they both crashed back into the Nile, sending waves flooding along the streets and creating thick clouds of sizzling steam. Seth floated above the river, looking to see if Horus would surface, but the river became flat once again and the air was quiet except for the ever-present heartbeat.

Seth tilted his head backwards and laughed. Twisting columns of pitch-black clouds erupted around him and winds whipped up a blinding storm of sand, smoke, ash and sparks.

Johnny was jolted back into action. 'Run,' he shouted, and they set off again. The Golden Ankh seemed heavier than before and Ted squeezed in between him and Yaz to help carry it. He sensed

Tutankhamun struggling to keep up, and urged the Pharaoh to carry on. They turned left into another street, losing sight of Seth and getting closer to the street with the Time Machine.

Yaz groaned in despair and Johnny nearly buckled at the knees. The Grand Vizier and his troops blocked their way at the far end of the street. His men glanced nervously at the God of Chaos.

Johnny couldn't hear Ay over the loud booming of the sky, the roar of the fire, and the rattle of flying sand, but he understood the gestures quickly enough. Ay ordered his soldiers to attack and they charged, screaming, towards them. The sand flew thicker and faster and, for a moment, the soldiers disappeared.

Johnny was sure they were about to die when Yaz shouted. 'Here's the next street to ours.' Johnny and Ted stumbled after her and almost dropped the ankh, but Yaz kept them upright and they staggered along the road. Johnny's arms ached with the weight of the ankh, his back was bent over and his skin stung from the sand.

Johnny realised Tutankhamun wasn't with them and he stopped. 'Where's Tutankhamun?' he shouted over the noise of the sandstorm.

'No idea,' replied Yaz, still trying to pull the ankh along the street. 'We can't look for him now.'

'We can't leave him,' insisted Johnny, refusing to

move.

'Let him go,' wheezed Ted.

'But he was just with us.' Johnny turned in the direction they'd come from but Yaz pulled Johnny towards the end of the street. 'Too late Johnny.'

He desperately peered through the sand but there was no sign of Tutankhamun. He let himself be pulled and pushed along by Yaz. How could they have lost him? He was there just a second ago.

The sandstorm cleared a little and Johnny realised how close the soldiers were behind them and he knew he had to give up on the Pharaoh. Their street was just a few steps away, they were close to safety, so he put his head down and ran as fast as he could, stumbling onwards. The deep thunderous sound of Seth grew louder again and the clouds were so dark it was almost like night. Buildings on either side of them shook so much that walls and roofs collapsed, and the three of them just managed to swerve past a large piece of wall that crashed into the road.

Screams made him look back to see Seth swooping low over the soldiers, sending a tornado that threw men into the air. Ay cowered with a small group of his guards in the doorway of the only house still standing. Seth rose back into the air with a clap of thunder and cry of frustration.

Desperately, Johnny, Yaz and Ted turned into

their street where, at last, they could see the Time Machine. They staggered on, the Golden Ankh getting heavier with every step as if a magnet pulled it down to the ground. The Time Machine's door was just a few steps away when another shout warned them that the Grand Vizier and his remaining men were chasing them again. The soldiers were moving much faster than Johnny, Ted and Yaz could manage, and Johnny pushed with his legs in one last-ditch attempt to reach the Time Machine.

Another shout from the soldiers distracted Johnny again and when he looked back this time, he saw Tutankhamun stand in front of Ay, his disguise cast aside. He held up his hands to signal them to stop and the Grand Vizier's men skidded to a halt. Johnny saw everyone bow down in front of Tutankhamun, except for Ay, who drew his sword and advanced on the Pharaoh before they once again disappeared in the swirling sandstorm.

More roofs blew away, scattering a storm of wooden posts, red tiles and chunks of plaster all around them. One post struck Yaz on her head, knocking her over, but she pushed herself back up, wiping a trickle of blood away from her face before lifting the ankh once more. Ted wheezed, his hands on his knees, as he tried to gulp air into his lungs. Johnny's stinging eyes filled with tears and he made one last effort to reach the Time Machine. Tutankhamun had sacrificed himself for them and Johnny had to make sure it was worthwhile.

30

The Sun God

The booming sound of the heartbeat grew agonisingly louder and Johnny saw the dark shadow of Seth swooping down towards them through the sand and ash, but once again he swerved away at the last moment. Seth tried again but something flung him high into the sky and he howled in anger. They were all on their knees now and Johnny knew they just had to keep crawling onwards in the hope they would reach the Time Machine before Seth caught them. He was painfully aware that Ted was wheezing more loudly and Yaz was bleeding where she had been struck by the wooden post. Tears streaked his face, his arms ached and his legs were numb. It wasn't fair, they were so close to the Time Machine, but they could barely move.

A white light came on and shone towards them from the direction of the Time Machine. It started as a faint point then widened and broadened into a bright beam that filtered through the sand, dust, ash, reeds and debris in the air. It was accompanied by an electronic hum that vibrated through the ground. Suddenly the light expanded to create a shimmering dome that pushed sand, smoke and even sounds away. They were kneeling inside a silent bubble of peace and tranquillity around them. Johnny blinked away sand and tears to see a figure standing at the door to the Time Machine. He was a brown-skinned man with the head of a hawk, dressed in a green and gold tunic, and the light came from an orb that hovered above his head.

'Ra?' wheezed Ted, clutching his chest. 'The Sun God?'

Yaz tried to sweep her hair away from her eyes but it was stuck to her face with blood and sand.

Seth circled ever higher above them, lightning-filled dark clouds swarming and billowing around him. Two more figures erupted from the clouds to hover on either side of the God of Chaos. Johnny recognised the coiling and writhing Apophis, the giant snake that had almost crushed Ted in Tutankhamun's tomb. The other beast looked like a hippopotamus with the claws of a lion and the tail of a crocodile. Johnny wondered what new type of monster this was, when Seth, Apophis and this new creature dived straight toward them. Johnny ducked and heard an ear-shattering bang. When he looked up again, the three gods were flying away as if they had hit the edge of Ra's light dome and simply bounced off. Cracks splintered around the dome and sand started to blow inside. Apophis uncoiled and slithered across the dome's surface, testing the cracks by striking at them with its fangs. Seth and the hippo-demon crashed again and again into the dome, which squealed with a piercing sound like rending metal and sent more sand raining down on them. Johnny was sure it would break at any moment. He glanced towards Ra, who was straining under the effort to keep the light around them. The Sun God's eyes were fixed on the top of the dome but he beckoned them on with his right hand.

'Come on,' urged Johnny, his voice little more than a whisper.

They began to pull and push the Golden Ankh slowly along the ground. The dome of light creaked and buckled with each ear-splitting attack. A screeching, gut-churning howl like a jet engine erupted above them and Johnny looked up to see three new figures streaking across the sky. A giant hawk, black cat and blue ram slammed into Seth, Apophis and the hippo-demon with an almighty crash and disappeared into a cloud of smoke, ash and sand.

Everything went quiet. Then Johnny watched, horrified, as Seth raised himself above the cloud and blew it away. The exploded remains of the other gods floated down like scraps of material. Seth bellowed and dropped onto the top of the dome, which sounded like a bass drum as it shook. The edge of the light started to flicker on and off.

Ra stumbled. 'Raise your hands, Jonathon, raise your hands.'

Johnny looked at the Sun God.

Ra lifted his arms higher up. 'You have the power to help me defeat Seth. You are a magician. Stand up, raise your hands. Use your power, Jonathon.'

Had he heard right? Ra was speaking to him? 'Only you can do this Jonathon. You have to do it now.'

Johnny struggled to his feet. He didn't think he had any strength left, but he did what the Sun God commanded and dragged his arms above his head to point at Seth. His legs started to tingle and shake once again with pins and needles. Johnny tried to concentrate and imagined striking Seth with a bolt of energy. His weariness washed away as the tingling turned into a surge of power that flowed through him from the ground to his hands. His whole body shook as arcs of fizzing, buzzing energy erupted from his fingertips like lightning bolts. With a deafening roar and a flash of searing light, they blew apart the storm clouds and smashed into Seth, who exploded. Johnny fell, exhausted, to his knees, while Ted and Yaz stared at him in astonishment. The dome of light flickered out. Sand, ash and burning reeds once again began to rain down on top of them.

'Come,' called Ra.

Johnny looked up and thought he saw the god step inside the Time Machine.

They all staggered to their feet, lifted the Golden Ankh and stumbled the last few steps into the Time Machine. Johnny had just enough strength left to slam the door shut behind him.

31

Almost Going Home

Johnny lay sprawled across the Golden Ankh, exhausted, aching and gasping for breath, yet relieved. They had all made it. Nearly all. Johnny was haunted by the sight of Tutankhamun standing in front of the soldiers. The Pharaoh had given his life to save them.

He looked around the Time Machine, expecting to see the god Ra lounging in one of the large red chairs but the room was otherwise empty.

'I expect gods can just disappear when they want to,' said Johnny.

When no one replied he looked at Ted and Yaz properly for the first time since their last encounter with the Sphinx. Yaz was bleeding and Ted was fighting for breath.

'Forget gods,' said Johnny as he struggled onto his feet to check who needed help first. Yaz was slumped in an armchair, her eyes half-closed and one hand clamped over the wound on her head, blood trickling between her fingers. Ted lay against the wall beside the door, trying to force air into his lungs, his eyes wide and white with fear.

Johnny didn't want to choose between his friends as he dragged the First Aid Kit from the other side of the room, flipped open the fasteners and lifted the lid. He basked in the cool, green, soothing light for a moment then moved it towards Yaz, who looked unconscious. He turned the dial to Heavy Bleeding. Once again, the calm electronic voice started speaking and the words appeared inside the lid. It did not waste time repeating the same introductions from last time, after Apophis. There was a sense of urgency about it.

'Let's not dilly-dally. Put the first patient's hand on the touchscreen immediately.'

Johnny guided Yaz's hand onto the milky glass disc and it glowed pale green once again while the First Aid Kit hummed.

'Oh dear, patient 4-5-1-9, you have been in the wars, haven't you? Diagnosis complete. Can one of her companions please stop her slouching?'

Johnny held Yaz up in front of the First Aid Kit.

'Do ensure her head wound faces the screen.'

Johnny gently turned Yaz's head to one side so that the bleeding was nearest the First Aid Kit.

'First and Emergency Aid for all Types of Atomic

and Molecular Injuries, Accidents and Near-Death Experiences will now conduct treatment,' spoke the First Aid Kit as the thin brass panels whirred, bleeped and clicked into place to bathe Yaz's head in green light.

Within seconds, the bleeding stopped, the dried blood faded away and her skin healed as if she'd not even had a scratch.

Yaz came around with a yelp. 'What's going on?' She sat backwards, rubbing her head where it had been bleeding.

'Oh, you know,' laughed Johnny in relief. 'Bit of first aid. You OK?'

'Never felt better,' replied Yaz, still looking surprised.

'Right, now for Ted.' Johnny wheeled the First Aid Kit over to Ted, who limply placed his hand on the touchscreen while Johnny selected Can't Breathe with the dial.

The kit sprang into life as soon as it felt Ted's hand. 'Tut, tut, patient 4-0-0-9 again. What have you been doing with yourself? Diagnosis complete.'

An ordinary, everyday-looking asthma inhaler popped out of the kit. Johnny was disappointed, expecting something more high tech, but Ted took a puff on it and his breathing returned to normal instantly.

'Wow, I've never been able to breathe so well,'

said Ted.

Johnny tried to close the First Aid Kit's lid, but it wouldn't budge. 'Not so fast, please place your hand on the touchscreen.'

'Me? But, I'm OK,' protested Johnny.

The First Aid Kit moved a little as if giving him a stern look, so he slowly did as he was told.

'Patient 4-5-2-0, you're the easy one but you do need a little tonic. I'll make some for all of you. Diagnosis complete.'

The bottles stacked around the touchscreen rattled as they rotated, and then three small, dark blue bottles rose on a little brass tray. Johnny picked up one and read the label.

'For general tiredness and wobbly legs. Take all in one gulp, put me back and have a nice day.' Johnny opened the bottle and sniffed the contents carefully. It smelled of coffee and old trainers. He held his nose and swallowed the whole lot in one go. He immediately felt invigorated and full of energy. After making Ted and Yaz drink the contents of the other bottles, he realised they had done it, they had escaped and they were all right. Johnny tried to push the image of Tutankhamun standing in front of Ay from his mind and concentrated on how they had rescued the Golden Ankh. He grinned at Ted and Yaz while he unwrapped the ankh to reveal the gleaming gold cross with its distinctive loop. He ran his fingers across the smooth, cool metal. They tingled and he felt a strong desire to own the ankh, which shocked him so much he snatched his hand away.

'We did it…' he began to say when there was a knock on the door.

Johnny's heart missed a beat as he leapt up and they all stared at the door in disbelief.

'Please let me in.' The words were weak and barely audible.

'Tutankhamun!' exclaimed Johnny as he wrenched open the door.

Tutankhamun fell forwards and Johnny caught him, dragged him to a chair and gently sat him down. Ted pushed the door closed from where he sat.

The First Aid Kit trundled over to the Pharaoh and opened its lid. 'This is urgent. Hand!'

Johnny placed Tutankhamun's hand on the screen, the First Aid Kit whirred, tutted and seemed to shake ahead, as if a box without a head could do that. 'Emergency transportation to New Haven Hospital required. Initiate procedure to return home now.'

Tutankhamun seemed to glow with the box's cool green light until he shrank and disappeared inside the First Aid Kit.

'What?' screamed Johnny.

'There is nothing to worry about. I have placed patient 1-3-3-2 inside a medical cocoon,' said the First Aid Kit, sounding smug. 'He will be safe there until I transfer him to New Haven hospital on our return.' With that, the First Aid Kit closed its lid and powered off.

The door now shook under a loud hammering.

'Break it down,' shouted the Grand Vizier from outside.

Ay's face appeared at the window. 'I can't see a thing.' He tried smashing the glass with his sword hilt, but it just bounced off. 'What is this? Come on, kick the door down.'

Each kick threatened to tear the door off its hinges.

'Home button,' said Ted as he stood up. He went to the globe, leant underneath and found the large red button set below the wooden ring next to the brass plate with the word 'HOME' on it.

As soon as Ted pressed the button, which made the most satisfying click, the globe came to life. The familiar continents faded from view to reveal the swirling red and yellow clouds, which moved faster and faster and soon mixed to form the surging mass of orange, while everything rattled and hummed loudly.

The door bent further than Johnny thought possible without actually breaking. Shafts of daylight and flurries of sand came in through the gaps that appeared every time the door was hit. Hurry up, he thought, clutching the Golden Ankh to his chest and backing away to the other side of the room. Johnny was sure the door would give in before the Time Machine left Egypt.

'What's that noise?' called Ay, just before his angry face and the view of Ancient Egypt disappeared from the window and the door stopped banging.

Johnny realised that they were on their way home with the Golden Ankh.

32

Return of the Ankh

When the Time Machine eventually creaked and shuddered to a halt, the swirling clouds had faded behind the map of the world, and the crazily clicking numbers clattered to a stop one last time at N-O-W, Johnny let out a huge sigh of relief. They were home. The hands on the grandfather clock pointed to a quarter past one in their time, which meant they were back just a little after lunchtime. Unbelievable, thought Johnny and felt instantly hungry. He also realised how dirty and unsuitably dressed for the twenty-first century they were in their slave clothes and coated with a thick layer of dust, ash and sand. They smelled slightly burnt.

'We really need a wash,' said Yaz. She grabbed a towel and her clothes as she went straight into the bathroom.

Johnny stood up with the Golden Ankh and expected Mr Merryweather to come through the door from the museum any moment, just as he had done after their previous trips, but the door stayed firmly shut. They had returned with the prize the Curator wanted, so why wasn't he bursting in, full of enthusiasm and congratulations?

'He'll be here soon Johnny,' said Ted. 'Come on, let's get the toast and marmalade down our necks then shower too. I really could do with getting this sand out of — well — everywhere.'

After a short while, they were clean and had eaten plenty of toast and marmalade. Johnny felt good and ready for Mr Merryweather to thank them. Where was he?

'Maybe he's busy with the others at Museum Club, you know how he always gives a talk after lunch.' Ted wiped toast crumbs from his mouth.

'Let's find him.' Johnny impatiently gathered the Golden Ankh in his arms and pushed open the door into the museum.

Yaz and Ted trooped after Johnny as he stomped towards the Buxton Room. The First Aid Kit zoomed out of the Time Machine, popped-up red emergency flashing lights and disappeared under a PRIVATE sign hanging from a chain stretched across a darkened corridor. It was another corridor Johnny was sure he hadn't seen before.

'I hope Tutankhamun's going to be OK,' said Johnny.

'He hasn't had his marmalade,' said Yaz.

'I wonder where it's going?' said Ted.

They almost bumped into Emily and Alisha.

'You've missed lunch,' said Alisha.

'Where's Mr Merryweather?' Johnny snapped back.

'Hello to you too Johnny. We don't know. We haven't seen him since he dashed out of the dining hall at the start of lunch.'

Johnny grunted and carried on.

'Charming,' Emily called after them.

'His office?' suggested Ted.

Johnny vaguely remembered that Mr Merryweather had an office somewhere, but hadn't paid any attention to where it was.

'This way.' Yaz set off down another corridor. 'I passed it when I broke in.'

They were soon standing outside a plain door. Its brass plaque read CURATOR in capital letters.

Ted cleared his throat. There was no reply, so he knocked quietly.

'Louder,' said Johnny.

Ted knocked again and, this time, they heard a faint sound of rustling on the other side of the door.

'Enter.' Mr Merryweather's voice just carried through the door, little more than a strained whisper.

Johnny looked quizzically at Ted, who

shrugged, then opened the door into a warm room, darkened with closed velvet curtains. It smelled overpoweringly of burning incense and sugary oranges. He could just make out the Curator reclining under blankets on a couch. Jars of half-eaten marmalade lay scattered across the floor. It looked as if someone had run amok, greedily scoffing as much marmalade as they could, as quickly as possible, from as many jars as they could find all at once.

Mr Merryweather slowly raised himself onto an elbow to look at them. 'You have returned.' He struggled to speak but the relief was evident in his faint, rasping voice.

Johnny almost dropped the Golden Ankh with worry. Was Mr Merryweather dying?

'I am sorry not to meet you in the Time Machine. It is unfortunate timing to be struck down with a migraine.' Mr Merryweather gingerly beckoned them towards him, and they carefully picked their way through the sticky jars. 'Please excuse the mess. Marmalade is also efficacious for inflictions of the neurological aura.'

'Mr Merryweather, sir?' asked Johnny hesitantly.

'What is it, Jonathon?'

Johnny thrust the Golden Ankh towards Mr Merryweather.

'You, you have the conductor?' Mr Merryweather carefully sat upright and allowed Johnny to place the bundle on his knees. He slowly opened the cloth with trembling hands and then gasped as the ankh's golden light lit up his face.

'Somebody likes butter,' murmured Yaz.

'My word, I wasn't sure if you would make it. Jonathon, Edward and Yasmin, you have done it, you have brought the Golden Ankh home.'

Johnny bristled at what sounded like surprise in Mr Merryweather's voice. 'What did you expect?' Johnny sounded more annoyed than he meant to.

'Oh Jonathon, I never doubted your resolve and abilities for one minute, but…' Mr Merryweather began to shake and sob.

'It's OK Mr Merryweather.' Yaz knelt beside him and spoke calmingly.

The Curator shook his head and wiped away tears. 'You, perhaps, do not know what this means to me. After all these years. It has been a long time since we last found a conductor. You have done the universe a great service. You are heroes beyond measure.'

Mr Merryweather took a deep breath and then leapt to his feet as if instantly rejuvenated. Johnny was amazed at how quickly the Curator's energy was returning and wondered how he could lift the heavy ankh so easily.

'We must have a celebration.' Mr Merryweather's eyes shone as he talked quickly and excitedly. 'With cakes and marmalade buns. Oh heavens, is that the time? There is a lot to do before you return to school. We will have a ceremony to replace the ankh in the Shield, then the party. Chop, chop!'

The Curator dashed out of his office; Johnny, Ted and Yaz looked at each other then rushed to follow. Mr Merryweather constantly congratulated them, admired the ankh and muttered, 'Wait until the others see this.' Johnny did not want to share the Golden Ankh with anyone else in Museum Club, this was special to him, Yaz and Ted only.

33

Shield Reunited

They entered the room with the Shield of Ages. Yaz gasped in astonishment when she saw the Shield glowing in the case at the far end of the room. This time its radiance slowly pulsed, as if it had a heartbeat. Mr Merryweather gathered them around the case and Johnny took in the large shining disc with its glinting jewels and intricate shapes and patterns.

'Before we return the Golden Ankh to its rightful place, I want you to recount everything that happened in Egypt — in summary form, of course.' Mr Merryweather looked at them over his glasses, his face shining with delight and gratitude. Johnny thought he looked like Father Christmas who had received all the presents.

Johnny told him as much as he could remember, Ted correcting him when he got his facts wrong and mispronounced names, while Yaz explained about her time as one of Ankhesenamun's slaves and their escape through the burning alleys. Mr Merryweather occasionally said 'remarkable' ... 'incredible' ... 'how is that possible?' He asked for detailed descriptions of Tutankhamun, the Sphinx and Seth, writing a few things about them in a small notebook, and said how he wished he could have been there to see it all with them.

When Johnny told him about Tutankhamun and the First Aid Kit, Mr Merryweather clucked in disappointment. 'What did I say about changing history?'

'It was Johnny's idea,' complained Ted.

'Well, I did hear an item on the lunchtime news about a new exhibition of Tutankhamun's treasure opening in Cairo. I am sure Ay found another body to bury as Tutankhamun's.'

Mr Merryweather asked them more and more questions until, eventually, he seemed happy with what they told him and put his thumbs behind the lapels of his jacket. 'This is very useful information, very helpful indeed for our future missions. You are all very brave and resourceful. You have confronted many dangers and overcome them with gusto. Congratulations. But there are some things to ponder. It would seem that the Shadow Lord was able to manifest Seth and use the God of Chaos for his own ends. Would you say that was possible?'

'I'm sure it was,' said Johnny.

'Yaz?'

'Don't know, could be,' she said.

'And what do you think Edward?'

Ted nodded. 'I didn't believe you before, but I've seen Ancient Egyptian gods and answered the Sphinx's riddles, so I guess I have to accept anything's possible now.'

'Good-o, Edward. We live in a rational world, where everything gets reduced to lifeless facts but, I hope, your adventure has shown you that science has much more to offer. The Shadow Lord's manifestation of Seth shows how weak the barrier must be between our two worlds. I wonder what he could do in Ancient Greece or China? What about the Sphinx, he was an interesting one, don't you think so?'

'Is he working for the Shadow Lord as well?' Johnny had disliked the Sphinx.

'I'm not so sure.' Mr Merryweather shook his head. A piece of straw or reed fell out. 'I suspect he saw an opportunity for mischief, perhaps glory. I doubt he was directly controlled by the Shadow Lord.'

'What about the knocking we heard from Ay's sarcophagus?' asked Ted.

'I may hazard a guess that Ay sensed your presence in the gallery and voiced his anger. There could be a physical memory of you all embedded in his mummy.'

'No way.' Ted's eyes widened in fear. 'That mummy has been dead for 3,000 years.'

'Well, not quite as long as that when we acquired him.' The Curator hummed a little tune.

'Hang on, do you mean you bot the mummies from Ancient Egypt too?' Ted looked shocked.

Mr Merryweather nodded.

'I thought you said you couldn't travel more than two hundred years ago!' said Ted.

'We had more staff until recently,' replied Mr Merryweather, sheepishly. 'Anyway Edward,' he quickly continued, 'I hope you now realise things are not always as clearcut as you may previously have thought.'

Ted sighed and Johnny grinned. That must be the understatement of the century.

Mr Merryweather beckoned them to gather around the Shield. It glimmered and rotated with new vigour as if it sensed it was about to be reunited with a part of itself. Mr Merryweather pressed a button underneath the side of the case and the glass slid away.

Johnny felt his heartbeat with the rhythm of the Shield's pulsing glow as he anticipated the Curator slotting the Golden Ankh into the waiting shape. It was a feeling of pride and happiness that he'd never known before.

'The honour of returning the Golden Ankh is yours, Jonathon, Edward and Yasmin.'

Yaz grinned enthusiastically. 'Too right!'

'But what if we drop it or put it in the wrong way?' said Johnny. 'I don't want to ruin the Shield's power.'

'Come on Jonathon, I know you are capable of reuniting the Golden Ankh with the Shield,' Mr Merryweather said encouragingly. 'All three of you have earned the right to do this.'

They lifted the Golden Ankh together, which now seemed so remarkably light and buoyant that it felt as if it was floating of its own accord. When they held it level with the Shield, the Shield pulsed with a brighter light and the ankh responded. Johnny felt the ankh begin to hum and vibrate the closer they moved it to the Shield, and his fingers started to tingle. When they held it above its space on the Shield he felt the ankh drift downwards.

'Gently does it,' urged Mr Merryweather, 'and get ready to let go when you feel the Shield pull on the ankh. When it locks on, the ankh will snap into place. It would be easy to lose a finger or two.'

It was as if a super magnet had switched on. They had just enough time to let go of the Golden Ankh as it slammed down into its place on the Shield. The ankh shimmered in and out of focus before settling into what felt like a high-resolution version of itself, while the Shield glowed a little more luxuriant than before.

Mr Merryweather clapped. 'It is done. This is a joyous day.'

Johnny, Ted and Yaz gazed in wonder at the Shield and the Golden Ankh, which they had risked everything for, had brought back through time from a distant land, fought the Grand Vizier's soldiers, been attacked by gods, and outwitted the Sphinx. Johnny blinked away tears, a lump in his throat, and put his arms around Yaz and Ted's shoulders. They had done it.

'Now, time for the celebratory tea I promised,' beamed Mr Merryweather. 'I have a rather special place to show you next week. I do believe it is time for you to visit New Haven.

Who's Who

This story is fiction based on real people of Ancient Egypt. Though they lived long, long ago, there is a lot we know about them but also much that we have not found out. There are some mysteries about what the main historical characters thought of each other. What they say and do is all my own imagination, based on what we know and some of what we don't know. The action is all in or near Luxor, called Thebes by the Ancient Greeks and Waset by the Egyptians. This is a wonderful place of temples, museums, the Avenue of the Sphinxes and the Valleys of the Kings and Queens.

Tutankhamun
Tutankhamun, also known today as King Tut, became Pharaoh of Egypt when he was only 9 years old. This was over 3,300 years ago, in 1,332 BCE. He ruled for 9 years until he was 18. His name means 'Living Image of Amun'. Amun was an important Egyptian god. Tutankhamun moved the capital of Egypt to Thebes, where he added new monuments to Karnak and Luxor temples. Tutankhamun was quite short and suffered from all manner of illnesses. Speculation over the cause of his death has included malaria, a fall, a blow to the head and sickle cell anaemia.

Grand Vizier Ay
Ay was a vizier — government advisor — to Tutankhamun. He is thought to have been the real power behind the throne. One Egyptologist believes that Ay murdered Tutankhamun in order to become Pharaoh himself. This claim is not

supported by other archaeologists or the x-rays of
Tutankhamun's mummy. Ay became Pharaoh after
Tutankhamun for four years.

General Horemheb

Horemheb was commander-in-chief of the army under
Tutankhamun and Ay. He was known for his ability to calm
Tutankhamun when the young Pharaoh's temper flared. He
became Pharaoh after Ay and ruled Egypt for 14 years.
During his reign he tried to remove all official records about
Ay, so he must have really disliked his predecessor.

Ankhesenamun

Ankhesenamun married Tutankhamun when he became
Pharaoh. She was 12 when they married, three years older
than him. They had two daughters, who died as babies, and
they did not produce an heir. It is thought that she then
married Ay.

Howard Carter

British Egyptologist Howard Carter is not an Ancient
Egyptian. He is famous because he rediscovered
Tutankhamun's tomb in 1922. It had hardly been raided by
tomb robbers so was full of more than 5,000 objects, including
the Pharaoh's gold funerary mask. That find became an
instant international sensation. Some of the objects are on
display in the Egyptian Museum in Cairo. The tomb is very
small for a Pharaoh. Some archaeologists think this is because
Tutankhamun died suddenly and had to be buried in a hurry,
others that Ay took over a grander tomb originally designed
for Tutankhamun. Some of the people involved in the
discovery of the tomb died soon after and this led to the belief
that they had been cursed by the Ancient Egyptian Pharaohs.

The Sphinx

The Sphinx was a mythical creature with the body of a lion and the head of a man. Egyptians thought of the Sphinx as benevolent, strong and a guardian. Sculptures of Sphinxes feature in many Egyptian temples, sometimes with the heads of Pharaohs. Long avenues of Sphinx sculptures guard the approaches to tombs and temples. The Great Sphinx of Giza is the most famous example and has become an emblem of modern Egypt.

Acknowledgements

Thank you to the people who have helped me while I wrote and published this book. Clare Fletcher, Mark Lilley, Georgia Litherland and Kaya Litherland have provided inspiration, encouragement, support and proofreading. I am especially indebted to the wonderful young readers who were the first to see the story and give me their feedback — Aiden, Amber, Amelia, Ephraim, Hunter, Kaya, Lila, Rosalyn, Stella and Verity.

If you have enjoyed reading this book, please review it on Amazon.co.uk or www.goodreads.com.

Thank you
Bill Bevan
April 2022

Printed in Poland
by Amazon Fulfillment
Poland Sp. z o.o., Wrocław

89193471R00160